CW01082776

# The Adventures of Crocco & Mr Noodlenutt

OTHER BOOKS BY CATHERINE BOND

*Moonmirror* (The Moon series, Book 1)

*Moonglimmer* (The Moon series, Book 2)

*Moonlighter* (The Moon series, Book 3)

*The Sparrow and the Mermaid*

# The Adventures of Crocco & Mr Noodlenutt

Catherine Bond

*The Adventures of Crocco & Mr Noodlenutt*

Published 2024

Book Publisher: Catherine Bond Books

© Text: Catherine Bond
email: info@catherine-bond.co.uk
website: www.catherine-bond.co.uk

© Illustrator Copyright: Jon Jacks

Catherine Bond and Jon Jacks assert the moral right to be identified as the author and illustrator of this work.

ISBN: 978-0-9957-942-4-5

*Conditions of sale*
This book is sold subject to the conditions that it shall not by way of trade or otherwise be lent resold hired out or otherwise circulated without the publishers written consent in any form of binding or cover other than that in which it is published and without a similar condition including this condition being imposed on the subsequent purchaser.

Typeset by The Book Typesetters
www.thebooktypesetters.com

# Acknowlegements

Grateful thanks to David and Suze
who listen and help.


*I dedicate this book to the memory of
Alan and Shirley Stewart, who were
good friends and talented artists.*

# Contents

## Adventure Three

## Adventure Four

# ADVENTURE ONE

## Chapter 1

# The Windmill

I magine you are standing on the shore beside a lake, one early morning in September. First you see a black pipe sticking up out of the water, and then you notice a big shiny bubble gradually rising to the surface. As you stare, a dark green object covered in warty spots rises up, and just when you are about to shout out in excitement, a long head with big round eyes and zig-zagged teeth appears. The creature starts to edge out of the water.

By now you are fixed to the spot, as the two eyes turn into bright headlights and an engine roars into life. What you thought were clawed legs gradually lift up to show four black wheels. There is a man's head in the bubble window – a head with a mass of twisted curly hair. Out of the water and onto the slipway slowly creeps an amazing crocodile-shaped car.

Mr Noodlenutt drove the car into a large boathouse on the edge of the lake. Inside there was a spacious workshop with tools and machinery which smelled of oil and old wood. Silently the garage door closed behind them. Crocco, which was the name of the car, sighed wearily as the old man opened the fuel cap and poured in a bottle of green, fizzy lemonade. Then he carefully wiped the car down, paying special attention to the bubble window in the roof, which made energy from the sun to power the lights and instruments.

This particular morning, somebody rang

the ship's bell hung in the doorway of Eight Bells Cottage, next to the boathouse. At once the door opened by itself, because Mr Noodlenutt had a piece of strong string attached to his foot which led to a pulley on the back of the door. It worked very well, as he didn't have to keep stopping his work to answer the door.

Dr Proctor stepped inside to see a figure wearing goggles with a gas torch alight, mending something on the bench. There was a strong smell of burning.

"Won't be a minute, Proctor. Make the coffee, will you?" came a muffled voice from behind the mask. "Oh, and get a couple of Danish pastries from next door, eh?" and the figure dressed in old overalls went back to work.

Dr Proctor and Mr Noodlenutt lived on opposite sides of the lake but although Goodly Harbour and Little Rushing by the Water were separated by water, they were joined together by a railway line. The lake was several miles long and the bridge across the lake saved a lot of time, instead of going round the long way or waiting for a ferry. Dr Proctor owned the train, a large American-style engine called *Trooper*, and drove it backwards and forwards all day long. He and Mr Noodlenutt were great friends and they had invented Crocco the submersible car together.

Dr Proctor put the kettle on and went next door. The bakery had a black-and-white striped awning to shade it from the sun and in the window were glass stands with chocolate cakes and sweets with rainbow-coloured papers and ribbons, strawberry tarts and creamy meringues piled high. He smiled at the delightful Mrs Magill who gave him two fat, warm pastries in a cake box and a bottle of green lemonade.

"I'll put it on the account," she nodded. "Day off, doctor?"

"Indeed, indeed, Mrs Magill, quite a treat."

"Very nice, it's going to be a lovely day," she smiled. "Just mind out later, there's going to be a thunderstorm."

Out of the corner of his eye, Dr Proctor

thought he saw a cake box fold itself up from a flat pile. Two tarts were placed into it by Mrs Magill. Then the roll of yellow ribbon on the wall wrapped itself around the box, even tying itself with a bow; but he thought he must be mistaken because it just wasn't possible.

The two old men sat in the autumn sunshine, eating delicious sticky pastries and drinking coffee. Dr Proctor only had two days off a year: today – his birthday – and Christmas Day. He could never remember how old he was but he had an ancient birthday card someone had sent him a long time ago which he got out every year. It seemed to make him happy.

"What would you like to do today?" Mr Noodlenutt asked his friend. "It's your birthday, you decide."

"I'd like a ride in Crocco up the lake and have a picnic beside the windmill," announced the doctor.

"Same as last year, then," said Mr Noodlenutt, smiling.

As they were putting the chairs away a

harbour launch came past the slipway, chugging up the lake.

"Morning, Lucas, morning, Jack," they called to it across the water.

The two uniformed figures standing in the front of the launch waved a reply. "We're checking up on any unauthorised boats moored up, now the summer's over," shouted the younger man. "Tell us if you see any without a sticker won't you? I'm going to tow them away."

"Will do!" and Dr Proctor gave them the thumbs up sign as they sped off up the lake in *Lionheart*, keeping the harbour launch carefully to the speed limit.

Captain Lucas Lively was the Harbour Master of Goodly Harbour and Jack was his bright, hardworking, young assistant.

"Just got to nip next door for something," and off went Mr Noodlenutt to collect the luxury picnic box he had ordered for a surprise birthday lunch. It was packed in brown cardboard and tied with whiskery string.

"You are a marvel, Mrs Magill."

He beamed at her, admiring her lovely brown curls and her clean flowery apron. She smiled back at him, saying nothing. Every morning he collected a bottle of green lemonade from her shop but he had noticed no one ever delivered green lemonade and he wondered where it could possibly come from. He had also noticed that only one sack of flour came from the mill now and again. It puzzled him how many cakes and pies could be made from just one sack of flour.

Returning to Crocco and Dr Proctor, he climbed into the driving seat and the car slid down the slipway and slowly entered the water. They were off!

# Chapter 2

# The Birthday picnic

In the square, the clock struck ten, loud and clear from the tower. It had a viewing balcony where people could stand and admire the view over the whole town. The clock saw everything that went on in Goodly Harbour and in Little Rushing by the Water. Even now it could see Sergeant Huff in the police station spreading blueberry jam on his morning toast.

It had already noted *Lionheart*, the harbour launch, motoring up the lake, and watched Jack rushing around making tea and biscuits, driving the boat, and talking on the radio to the harbour office. He could see the captain settling down for a snooze against the cosy cushions and leaving everything to Jack, as usual.

Yes, the clock saw everything, ticking away, chiming perfectly; never looking back, the clock's hands inched life forward in all seasons and weathers, happy in its important work of keeping Goodly Harbour on time.

In the police station, Sgt Huff had finished his breakfast. As Goodly Harbour only needed one police officer, Sgt Huff and his wife lived in the police house above the station. Its timbered rooftop looked out over the lake and Mrs Huff had cheered it up with window boxes of red geraniums. Sgt Huff was a grumpy man who never smiled and complained constantly that the wretched flowers blocked his view and got in the way of his 'observations'. He had a large shiny pair of binoculars on a stand, situated on the front balcony, so that he could observe everything that went on and write it down in his white notebook.

"My notes will come in very handy one day, Mrs Huff, you mark my words. My superiors will be impressed with my dedication when we have an incident of major importance. I'll have it all written down," and he puffed himself up imagining the praise that would be heaped upon him – diligent Sgt Huff.

"Yes dear," agreed Mrs Huff, "right as always," and she went downstairs, took out another of the white notebooks from the cupboard beside the fireplace and lit the fire with it.

"There now, that's got it going." She knelt back in satisfaction and then gave the fire a gentle prod with the poker. "That's another one I've got rid of – only 213 left to go."

Sergeant Huff scanned the lake with zeal. He could see *Lionheart* the harbour launch disappearing slowly.

"There's that lazy Lucas lolling about again and poor old Jack hard at it." He sucked his teeth. "I'll be the one that catches any criminals on this lake, you wait and see."

Next he saw Crocco motoring by, the glass bubble visible above the surface and two heads clearly to be seen inside.

"Huh!" Sgt Huff made a face and rolled his eyes, "Those two crackpots again and that ridiculous excuse for a car or a boat or whatever it is. I wonder if he needs a special licence for that machine? I'd better check. They might be breaking the law. Yes indeed, I just might get that thing banned," and he smiled nastily at the very idea.

Sgt Huff did not like Mr Noodlenutt or Dr Proctor. They were too inventive and far too pleased with themselves for Sgt Huff's liking. He didn't understand people who were always trying to change things. What was wrong with things as they were? It was all an annoying threat to Sergeant Huff's ordered life.

"No regard for authority, especially mine. That's what's wrong with those two," he told himself. "Now… where are they off to?" he wondered. "Interfering again in something, no doubt."

He watched as the car gradually submerged. Only the black pipe was left on the surface.

"Huh, better signal the colonel. He'll tell me if they've passed him upstream."

He got out his pocket torch with its extra bright signalling button and proceeded to flash Morse code in the direction of Colonel Boodle-Smith's house.

The message read after ten warning flashes:

*TARGET APPROACHING.*
*OBSERVE. REPORT P.M.*

Colonel Boodle-Smith, his wife Queenie and their dog Major lived on the Little Rushing side of the lake. He had retired from a busy life in the army but was still a very active jolly man, enthusiastic about everything and liked a bit of excitement. He also disapproved of new-fangled ideas, as he told Sgt Huff one day, and the two instantly bonded into like-minded friends.

"Any help I can give you apprehending ruffians, sergeant, I will. Just call on me. We must keep this town ordered and well disciplined, that's the key, don't you see?"

Sgt Huff agreed wholeheartedly, glad of someone at last who thought like him. Between them they had begun a Morse code signalling system to report and observe life in the whole area. Each had a call sign and times to operate. Col Boodle-Smith took it all very seriously, dressing in his combat uniform if he was involved in anything connected with police work. He owned a small boat called *Duty*, a lovely varnished wooden motor launch moored up at the foot of his lakeside garden.

That morning he received Sgt Huff's signal as he sat in his large sun room reading the *Times*. His call signal, the letter B, flashed in his window. He jumped up knowing Sgt Huff would repeat it five minutes later. Notepad at the ready he waited, then *TARGET APPROACHING. OBSERVE. REPORT P.M.*, read the colonel, carefully counting the flashes.

"Righty ho. Will do," and he rushed to the window where his army telescope was waiting on the table. He snatched it up, pulled on his combat jacket and an old blue beret and charged down to the garden in his tartan slippers, scattering the ducks as he went. He reached the wooden pontoon and hurried onboard his boat. It rocked wildly as he entered and sat down heavily puffing and panting. He was rather overweight and enjoyed perhaps one too many of Mrs Magill's famous pies. Finally he settled himself and concentrated on scanning the lake.

"Target approaching, eh? Probably that tin can of Noodlenutt's. Got to look for that damned periscope thing on the top. Hard to see against the black water," he muttered to himself. "Message was received at 10.30. Should be very close now depending on the speed. Ah, what's this? Steady now, steady the Buffs! Gotcha! Target located." He glanced at the ship's clock on the wall. It was 10.45 a.m., heading in a northerly direction, and he followed it closely with his eye.

"Six knots, I'd say." Pleased with himself, he put the telescope down with a triumphant sigh and opening a low cupboard nearby he took out a small glass and a large bottle and poured himself a ruby red measure of sloe gin. Then he opened a tin of Mrs Magill's best butter shortbread and enjoyed an early morning treat. He then reviewed the lake for a while until the telescope slipped from his hand, and he lay back against the canvas cushions and fell asleep.

When the phone rang in the house five minutes later, a caller wished to speak to the colonel. Queenie answered in her best voice: "I'm so sorry, he's on *Duty* at the moment." Because that was exactly where he was – fast asleep on his beloved boat aptly named *Duty*.

In the crocodile submersible car, Mr Noodlenutt turned the headlights on so that Dr Proctor could enjoy life under the lake. He was fascinated as they passed bits of people's rubbish rusting on the bottom, and the hubbub of the watery world that went by. Mooring ropes and buoys made shadows on the surface and flashes of sunlight lit up the grey-green water. There was not a single sound except Crocco's engine.

"Would you like to drive?" asked Mr Noodlenutt kindly.

"Oh, could I?" beamed Dr Proctor. "Show me the controls again."

It was very easy: one pedal and one steering wheel, one lever – fast, slow, stop, reverse. The green lemonade fizzed around the pipes and little bubbles of gas escaped through the exhaust. A red button made the periscope higher or lower and the depth of the water above and below them was registered on the screen in red. The bubble dome on the roof of the car had two doors especially designed not to let water in and two doors on the bottom of the car for use when Mr Noodlenutt climbed out during an underwater operation. A button marked LADDER operated the sliding ladder to climb up and out of the bubble when necessary. Crocco could operate all the coloured buttons himself with a voice recognition system when Mr Noodlenutt needed him.

After three quarters of an hour they were almost at Higher Rushing. There was a map of the lake under glass beside them and a tiny green light showed them where they were. The red button switched on and the periscope began to lower. Mr Noodlenutt took over as he could see the windmill up in front of him and the small beach area where the slipway was.

Then very gradually the round shiny bubble appeared on the surface and the dark green warty body of Crocco rose out of the water and the wheels took over from the clawed paddles. Water streamed off the crocodile car as the engine revved, and the whole amazing vehicle drove slowly onto the shingly beach and up the hill to the windmill.

The big wooden mill had been working for over a hundred years, grinding grain into flour between its powerful revolving stones. Dusty Dave was the miller, who worked every day pouring brown sacks of grain into the mill and collecting soft flour in white sacks at the other end. The large sails of the windmill turned creakily in the wind, attached inside to a giant spindle which powered the mill. At the top of the hill where the windmill had been built you could look down the lake for miles, and it was of course as you would expect, very windy up there.

The farmers from all around brought their wheat and corn to the mill and it was from this flour that Mrs Magill made all her lovely bread and cakes.

Next to the windmill was a grassy field set about with picnic tables and seats. Dusty Dave had made a play area for children, who don't want to sit still or look at the view. This spot was where Mr Noodlenutt and Dr Proctor had planned to eat their lunch.

Dusty Dave looked out of the window and waved. He seemed a very old man indeed, but when he came out to greet them it was obvious that Dusty Dave was covered from head to toe in flour dust. He looked so old because of his white hair, but in reality he was quite a young man.

"Morning, Mr Noodlenutt, and Dr Proctor." He nodded to each of them, starting to cough as the wind swirled the dust around.

"Come and get some fresh air with us," said Dr Proctor kindly, "we've brought lunch."

The wind blew fiercely at the top of the

hill and beneath the windmills blades they spread the marvellous picnic out on a wooden table and admired it. Cold duck, chicken and pigeon layered pie, tomatoes and a leafy salad. Crusty warm bread, fingers of cheese, fat green olives, and a box of sticky gooey chocolate brownies. There was a small bottle of green lemonade for Crocco and a large bottle of curious black fizzy stuff for the others: Mrs Magill's special elderberry and dandelion brew. A birthday cake with blue icing and one blue candle sat at the very bottom, and a tiny box of matches.

"Well, what a treat!" Dr Proctor was very excited and got out the plates, glasses and cutlery from the box. Big grey clouds appeared on the horizon suddenly and spread across the sky.

"Looks like rain. Come on, let's eat before it starts." Said Dusty Dave looking up and frowning.

They tucked into the delicious picnic and finally lit the blue candle, singing Happy Birthday to the doctor, who beamed with happiness.

"Thank you," he said quietly.

Just then a large drop of rain landed on the candle and it went out; it was followed by many more, but the candle relit itself.

"Quickly, come and shelter in the windmill," suggested Dusty Dave, and they hurriedly packed the remains of the picnic away. Dr Proctor carefully held the blue candle which would not go out no matter how many times he blew on it.

By the time they got inside the door and up the staircase, the rain was belting down, huge black clouds covered the sky and the thunder and lightning began.

The windmill's blades creaked loudly as the wind pushed them round. Through the window, sheets of rain and gashes of bright lightning flashed across the water. In a nearby corner of the lake was the other building at Higher Rushing. A huge waterfall gushed off the mountains nearby and situated below it was the hydro-electric power station. This large old brick building used the rushing waters to turn a turbine which created electricity which was then stored and sent down the valley to the two villages of Goodly Harbour and Little Rushing by the Water. The power station was a very important place, responsible for all the lights in the homes and streets and everything else that worked by electricity.

Higher Rushing was a lovely place, surrounded by tall, rocky mountains, pine trees, green mossy secret places and always, always, the roar and swish of tumbling foaming water. Only two people lived there, the men who ran the power station day and night, Bill Brightly and Sparky Watts. They were both electrical engineers who loved their work and enjoyed living in the big power station with the views of the windmill and the vast lake. In the distance they could just see the bright glow of Goodly Harbour when it got dark, and it gave them a great feeling to know it was all because of them that the lights came on faithfully each evening.

They stood in the upper room looking out at the violent storm that had arrived so quickly and reduced their view to a dark hazy rain-gashed circle around the power station, occasionally lit up by a flash of head aching lightening.

"Cor! That was a big one!" gasped Sparky, shielding his eyes from a brilliant fork of light. Thunder roared again.

"Watch out, another one coming!" Bill warned him, and a few moments later several flashes and then one long one seared the sky; with a loud crack one of their connections outside was struck violently and blew up in a smoky ball of light. The small fire was immediately put out by the driving rain, hissing and spluttering as it did.

"Oh no! That's done it," groaned Sparky, holding his head.

Bill looked very worried indeed. He peered through the rain and clouds at the connection which lay in pieces, smoking. He knew at once the electricity had stopped flowing, broken by the huge strike of lightning. Everything they had always worked so hard to prevent had happened – a power cut, their biggest nightmare.

# Chapter 3

# The Power cut

Down in Goodly Harbour, everything very slowly came to a stop. People were puzzled at first, and some things weren't even noticed. Col Boodle-Smith was alerted by Queenie who couldn't get her hairdryer to work. Then the radio went off during her favourite programme. It was nearly 2.30 p.m., so when the colonel replied to Sgt Huff's message, he gave his call sign and sent his news: *TARGET PASSED UPSTREAM. SIX KNOTS AT 10.45 A.M. POWERCUT HERE. ON WATCH. B.* He flashed his Morse code message towards Goodly Harbour.

Sgt Huff checked the lights and his TV at home and down in the station. All dead.

"Dear oh dear, that's serious. Power cut? Just the time for burglars to strike, tonight!" There were only a few hours of daylight left.

Sparky Watts and Bill Brightly rushed out of the power station. The rain and wind took their breath away; neither had bothered to get a coat and they stood looking at the blackened smoking metal connections, scratching their chins and thinking hard, soaked to the skin in minutes.

"Have to bypass it, Bill."

"You're right, Sparky, it's the only answer."

But how? remained the question.

Dr Proctor seeing the two engineers out of the rain splattered window, hurtled down the wooden stairs holding firm to his blue unquenchable birthday candle, and ran outside.

"Dr Proctor! Where'd you spring from?"

"Oh, we're sheltering. Come on up and have some tea. Come on!" He encouraged them, beckoning, "Come on in out of this rain!" And they followed him inside the big spacious mill.

Sitting up there with the windmill blades creaking round and round, it was eerie and dark for early afternoon.

Dusty Dave passed a tray of tea to Sparky and Bill and Dr Proctor offered some birthday cake. They munched silently, thinking hard and trying to solve the problem. Several minutes went by, the candle glowing brightly as it had been stuck back into the remaining icing – Mrs Magill's cakes, all made with her special flour had been known to have magical effects on some people, often just at the right moment.

"I know!" they suddenly all spoke together, pleased and excited, one finger raised in the air.

"Got an idea!" and everyone did exactly the same thing at exactly the same time. They started to talk over each other as the ideas started flowing.

"How about this?"

"This is a great idea!"

"What if we do this?"

"I've got a good plan, why don't we…"

"*Stop!*" roared Mr Noodlenutt, exasperated, "One at a time, gentlemen please," and silence fell.

"Right Sparky, you first." Mr Noodlenutt nodded at him.

"I was thinking we could run a cable and bypass the break down at number 2 pylon but it's a bit rocky on that side and we'd need a good climber. The cable is heavy, but it could be done, couldn't it?" he faltered, "Maybe?"

"Bill, you next."

"I thought we could rig up a dynamo, temporary like, from the windmill, and we could make enough power for some lights up here to make repairs to the connection. Doc?"

"I had the same idea about the windmill. Use the wind power to drive a dynamo! Great minds think alike, eh?" Doctor Proctor very pleased with himself.

"I wonder if Crocco and I could take the

cable down to the second pylon?" added Mr Noodlenutt, "*but*, under the lake. Seems much easier than climbing along those rough rocky edges. The pylon has a ladder to reach the connectors. Sparky and Bill can do it easily. What about that?"

All were dumbstruck for a moment.

"Excellent! Good idea. I think it will work. Great plan," they all chipped in together.

"More cake?" offered Dr Proctor, and they ate happily until every crumb was gone and only the candle remained, burning brightly.

"Let's get the lights rigged up first," suggested Dr Proctor, "then everyone can see what's going on."

"How you gonna do that then?" asked Dusty Dave rather anxiously.

"Come and watch," suggested Dr Proctor and they trooped down the winding wooden staircase to the flour bagging areas, where the big cogs were turning. The doctor rubbed his chin, thinking.

"I might have to disconnect the windmill

from the grinder for a bit. Will you mind, Dave? Only for a couple of hours, won't take long."

He held up the small blue perpetual candle to see the miller's face. Dusty Dave looked worried.

"Long as my windmill's working by the morning it's alright with me," was his brave decision.

"Now gentlemen, Dave is relying on us, let's get up to the top, disconnect the spindle and set up the dynamo. Bring up some cable and lights. Okay?" and the doctor organised the whole thing.

Dave watched the mysterious goings-on of the two skilled electrical engineers and Dr Proctor. Suddenly, two large spotlights were being attached to the outside of the building as if by magic. The large blades of the windmill continued to turn in the strong wind. The rain had eased back to a steady fall. Things were beginning to happen.

Bill and Sparky returned to the power station to prepare their large connectors and the supply cable for its transportation down the lake. Bill remembered to first switch the large main lever to OFF.

The lights on the windmill had not gone unnoticed. Col. Boodle-Smith had seen them shining through the murky gloom and he took a closer look with his binoculars.

"By Jove, something's afoot up the lake, Queenie. Try our lights again, will you?"

But disappointingly they did not come on. Col Boodle-Smith chased down onto his boat once again and signalled to Sergeant Huff, giving his call sign.

*LIGHTS AT WINDMILL.*
*SHALL I INVESTIGATE.*

Sergeant Huff couldn't see the lights form where he was so he had to rely on the colonel's information as correct. He too tried his lights but they didn't work. He had decided to go on foot patrol that night in the darkness and was unhappy about leaving the town. Who knew what villains might be lurking in the streets to rob and commit crimes against the unsuspecting inhabitants of Goodly Harbour?

"No, my place is here," he told himself firmly, "I must do my duty. Boodle-Smith can go and investigate. He'll be a match for anyone in a fight with all that army training."

So Sgt Huff sent a Morse code message back.

*YES INVESTIGATE. NO
HEROICS. REPORT BACK
A.S.A.P.*

The colonel was delighted. He dressed in his combat clothes, smeared his face with camouflage grease and set off with all speed in his motor launch. He left Queenie happy beside the fire with some candles and a plate of chicken sandwiches.

"Lovely, peace at last," she chuckled. "What a treat!"

Sparky Watts and Bill Brightly had carefully sorted and collected everything they needed but safety was their first priority. Electricity could be exceedingly dangerous.

The cable was attached to a towing hitch on Crocco's rear bumper. Mr Noodlenutt would drive to the second pylon past the power station. Dr Proctor stayed with Dusty Dave to manage the lights and point them in the right direction. The two electricians got into the car with Mr Noodlenutt and as it entered the dark water from the shingly beach, Crocco turned his lights on. Sparky and Bill, feeling very nervous about being under the water, were amazed and excited by the amazing car. Crocco revved the engine to pull the extra weight of the cable and gently manoeuvred it to the steep edge of the lake at the foot of the chosen pylon.

"Put one of those rubber suits on and a hood, there's several hanging up behind us," ordered Mr Noodlenutt. They dressed, put their own boots and gloves on and strapped their tool bags onto their backs.

The bubble roof breached the surface and the special valve opened. The ladder was centralised and out climbed the two brave engineers into the darkness, getting a good foothold on the rocks beside them.

It wasn't dark for long, as Dr Proctor and Dusty Dave watching with binoculars for Crocco's lights knew when they had reached their destination and turned the spotlights towards the top of the pylon. Mr Noodlenutt got into his suit, left by the exit and went to the back of the car, untied the cable and hauled it into the arms of the waiting engineers. Tying the end to themselves, they started the slow steep climb up to the pylon's connectors in the driving rain and strong wind, hardly able to see with the water in their eyes. Both were nervous and shaking, but tried to overcome their fears, and not think about falling.

Dr Proctor had instructions to go to the power station and double check that the MAINS POWER switch was off. This was extremely important and he did it at once. Everyone had to be very patient while Sparky and Bill got on with their work. Reconnecting and joining up the large cable to its glass connectors with special tools took time. All was silent, just the clinking of the tools against the metal and the shrieking and wailing of the wind. It was almost as if the wind was trying to dislodge them.

Along the rocks somebody was creeping up closer and closer, watching and wondering what was going on. Col Boodle-Smith had landed his boat further down the lake and was proceeding on foot. His eyesight wasn't good now and neither was his hearing. He struggled in the driving rain, constantly wiping his eyes and tripping occasionally over the rocks, now wet and slippery. He hadn't seen Bill or Sparky climbing up but he had seen the lights up the pylon. Suddenly Sparky dropped his large spanner from his hand – blonk, blonk, tickety, tap, tap, tap, – down it went, hitting the pylon on its way, clanging loudly.

"What was zat?" hissed the colonel to himself and stopped dead in his tracks.

Sparky sighed, disappointed with his mistake, knowing he would have to go all the long way down again said, "I'll have to go and get my spanner, Bill. Just wait a minute for me will you?"

"Okay."

He began the climb down into the

darkness below. As he reached the bottom at last he trod on the colonel, who gave a mighty roar. They fell over in the darkness, struggling with each other both frightened and angry. Poor Sparky was no match for the colonel, who had been a jungle fighter and landed a few good punches, grabbing Sparky by the neck in a fierce grip.

"You're coming with me, you saboteur!" and he bundled and pushed the frightened man along, arms behind his back, poking an old gun in his ribs convinced he was the one who had cut the powerlines. Sparky was unable to understand what had happened but this bloke scared him and had a gun. He might shoot him. In no time he was thrown into *Duty* waiting by the water and tied up. Col Boodle-Smith started the engine and chugged back down the lake terrifying Sparky with threats of what tortures and ill treatment he had in store for him if he misbehaved. As he had gagged the poor unfortunate electrician it was not possible to tell the Colonel of his terrible mistake.

Bill, waiting up the pylon, heard some

noises but couldn't see anything. He shouted to Sparky but there was no answer. Crocco heard the roar of *Duty*'s engine through the water.

Bill was puzzled. What was Sparky doing? It was cold up there in the rain. He decided to go down and investigate but when he got to the bottom of the pylon there was nothing. Shining in the cleft of a rock was the big silver spanner. Where was Sparky?

Mr Noodlenutt, opening the hatchway called out. "What's wrong?"

"Sparks is missing."

"Can't be!"

"He's gone. I tell you he's not here," insisted a tense Bill. "Now who'll help me?" and he shook his head. "I can't fix this without Sparky. Nobody else can do it."

"I will," offered Mr Noodlenutt. "Come on, just show me."

He started to climb up the pylon with Bill and the spanner. Bill had no choice. The job had to be completed and so in the end by the light from the windmill, buffeted by the wind and relentless rain, the two brave men succeeded in bypassing the first break in the line and making a new connection. They would only be able to tell if it worked when the MAIN SWITCH in the power station was switched on. Bill was determined it was going to be him that pushed the switch. What could have happened to poor Sparky Watts? Had he fallen into the lake? No one had heard anything. He didn't know he was now a prisoner of Col Boodle-Smith.

The colonel was shaking with excitement and glee. He'd caught the saboteur who had cut the powerlines. Dressed like that, he'd meant business alright. Wait until Sgt Huff took a look at him. He'd tied a spotted handkerchief around his mouth to stop him talking, but Sparky continued to struggle and make noises.

*Duty* headed straight for Goodly Harbour and the police station which was by the jetty. The colonel neatly berthed the boat alongside and tied her up, then he pulled Sparky to his feet.

"Come on you piece of no-good stinking meat, get your carcass over here!" and he pushed him up the steps and over to the police station.

Sgt Huff was exhausted. He had been patrolling the streets every hour searching for burglars, murderers and bank robbers but had caught no one and was just returning for a nice cup of tea. He saw Col Boodle-Smith in front of him. Whatever was he doing? And who on earth was that dressed in a diving suit? He broke into a run.

"Boodle-Smith? Is that you?" and they all reached the police station door together.

"Prisoner for you, Sgt Huff!" beamed the colonel. "He's the one who cut our powerline I'm pretty sure, dressed like that. Up to no good, eh?" and he poked Sparky in the chest with his old pistol. Sparky struggled and tried to speak making some very strange noises behind his gag.

"Now, now, into the interview room. Then tell me all about it in there."

Sgt Huff opened the door and straightened his uniform, took off his hat and called to Mrs Huff to make some tea. Then he lit two candles and sat the wet bedraggled, bound and gagged prisoner in front of him.

"I'm not taking that gag off until I hear what Col Boodle-Smith has to tell me, alright?" Sgt Huff told him, looking at the hooded and gagged face. Had he seen him somewhere before? Was he amongst the wanted photos of criminals he was sent every week? Quite possibly. Maybe he would apprehend a dangerous murderer and be given a medal? How wonderful that would be! Sparky nodded that he would give no trouble. He was too tired, cold and wet to argue. It was all a nightmare.

"Quite a simple operation, Huff. Arrived at the lake edge, moored my craft, saw that strange light centred on a new position. All set up for this dastardly deed no doubt. Followed it, apprehended a suspect, immobilised him and brought him to base for interrogation. Now it's over to you civilians, what? Do you need me? Can you manage him alone?"

Col Boodle-Smith hadn't had such an exciting job for years. Imagining himself colonel of the regiment again, he was rather rude to Sgt Huff.

"Em, thank you colonel, actually I think

it best if you go now. I shall deal with this."
And he opened the door and directed him out.

"Oh, what? Go? Oh, alright old boy! Be
in touch, not a problem."

And he left the police station and made
towards his boat moored up on the jetty. He
roared off home to tell Queenie all about it.

Mrs Huff brought the tea downstairs into
the interview room just as the lights came on
all over the town. Sgt Huff had untied poor
Sparky's hands, removed his gag and was
helping him pull off his black rubber hood.
By now Sparky was aware of the lights on and
smiled to himself. Well I never! Proctor and
Noodlenutt did it! Good old Bill!

"Hello, Mr Watts! What are you doing
here? My goodness, you don't look too good, if I
may say so. Here's a nice cup of tea for you and
I'll get you something to eat. Poor man! What
have you been doing to him, Huff old dear?
Don't you know Sparky Watts when you see
him, huh?" She gave Sparky his tea and glaring
at her husband, flounced out of the door.

Sgt Huff sat down wearily, took a cup of
tea off the tray, had a few sips and looked in

horrified silence at Mr Watts from the hydro-electric station. Of course he recognised him now, with the hood and gag off. He shivered. What on earth had happened?

"You'd better tell me all about this, Mr Watts. There seems to have been a bit of a mistake."

Mrs Huff returned with a bowl of thick, steaming soup for Sparky and nothing for Sgt Huff. He really was in the doghouse. Ten minutes later the policeman and his prisoner were driving along in the big, black, shiny police car all the way round the lake to deliver Sparky Watts home. Well, it was the least Sgt Huff could do after he had heard the story, and wasn't Col Boodle-Smith in trouble? Assault, abduction, arrest - enough to bring a court case against them all, but dear old Sparky was just happy that the lights had been restored. He did wonder, however, how Bill had managed to connect it all up without him. No, he didn't want to press charges but he had one thing to say to Sgt Huff.

"I don't think the colonel should run about with that toy gun, sergeant, he might go frightening people. Some folks might think it's real, you know."

"It *is* real, Sparky, he's had it since he left the army. 'Course it's against regulations, but you know the colonel, he gets carried away. Doesn't mean any harm, he's just trying to help. Takes him back to his good old army days. He's promised to lock his gun away now. Probably doesn't work anyway." He coughed nervously.

Sparky felt quite faint all of a sudden. He would be glad to get home, and he leaned against the leather seats and closed his eyes. Job done.

Back at the windmill, Bill and Dr Proctor were putting the spindle back, taking away the dynamo and getting ready to grind flour again. Dusty Dave and Mr Noodlenutt were making a celebration dinner for Sparky's return. Sgt Huff had telephoned them and given them the good news. With his own flour, Dusty Dave made a great big pizza and put it in the oven. It was covered in cheese, ham, tomato, pineapple and pepperoni and was going to be very good indeed.

At last, the windmill was back to normal. The electricity was being made by the turbines in the power station, Sparky arrived home, and everyone was happy except Sgt Huff. He had to tackle Col Boodle-Smith and try to get him to apologise. Then he had to make peace with his wife or he would get no supper. Ahh, life wasn't easy as the town's only policeman. Nobody appreciated his dedication. He sniffed sadly, feeling rather sorry for himself. If only it had been a real criminal he would have been a hero.

Supper at the power station was a jolly great feast and Dr Proctor enjoyed yet another birthday celebration. Bill and Sparky were pleased with all their hard work and they agreed it had all been achieved by splendid teamwork.

Later that evening Crocco, Mr Noodlenutt and Dr Proctor motored down the lake in the moonlight, staying on the surface this time, following the lights to Goodly Harbour. Dr Proctor was full of thanks for his busy day.

"I haven't enjoyed a birthday as much as

this since last year," he told Mr Noodlenutt. "Let's do it again sometime."

"That'll be next year then," replied his friend.

"Yes, yes that will do and I have plenty of time to think about it. Great fun. I think we did a little bit of good today, don't you?" and he went off whistling, back to *Trooper* his train who was waiting patiently in the railway station yard. In his pocket only the burnt-out stub of the blue candle remained; it had at last gone out.

Crocco, using the last few drops of green lemonade, sank into his cosy garage and closed his eyes. What a day!

Mr Noodlenutt lit his pipe and sat on the quayside, puffing away in the dark as the moon played hide and seek behind the clouds. He thought back on everything that had happened.

Next door, Mrs Magill watched him for a moment from her bedroom window, then she pulled the curtains, and smiling to herself, turned off the light. Some birthdays were magical, she thought, as she drifted off to sleep, and why shouldn't Dr Proctor's be one of them?

# ADVENTURE TWO

## Chapter 4

# Babychino runs away

Now, perhaps it's time to tell you a little more about the other people who live in Goodly Harbour and Little Rushing by the Water. One other very popular shop was Mr Rocadello's Ice Cream Parlour. He made all his own delicious ice cream in so many different flavours it was hard to choose.

In the summer holidays the children would

queue outside waiting for their turn, and each year there were new flavours to try. You could also have extra toppings: chocolate sprinkles, chocolate, raspberry and caramel sauce, fluffy squirted cream, crunchy chopped nuts, red cherries and pretty rolled wafers, all waiting in little dishes to put on yourself. Dainty metal tables and chairs stood outside where you could sit and enjoy an ice cream with friends.

All the milk and cream for the ice cream came from Bilberry Farm near Higher Rushing. Mr Rocadello's cousin Cosmo ran this farm with his wife, Maria. They kept a herd of pretty-faced Jersey cows who gave wonderful creamy milk and the couple worked every single day, morning 'til night looking after them, because cows have to be milked twice a day, washed and kept clean, fed and watered.

Maria made a special hard, salty cheese and she had her own barn with lots of wooden shelves to store the big rounds. The farm milk was sent down to Mr Rocadello twice a week in their red van with a cow painted on the side. Cosmo always stopped to have a coffee and sometimes he tasted the new flavours. Sometimes he didn't like them. Mr Rocadello would listen quietly, nod his head, then decide what to do. Quite often Cosmo was right if he didn't like it, say, prunes and custard ice cream… Mr Rocadello would find that if he put it out for sale, nobody else liked it either. So he learned to listen to his cousin very carefully.

In the autumn the last calves were born at Bilberry Farm and the mother cows stood proudly feeding their little calves, who were the prettiest you could ever see. Maria gave all her cows names; her favourite was Toffee Nose. Her calf was creamy white and coffee-coloured so Maria called him Babychino. The farm was extremely busy that week and that is probably how Maria forgot a very important thing one day.

Cosmo loaded up the milk cans and drove off in the red van to Goodly Harbour. Maria went to check her cheeses, feed the cows and calves, wash the floor and put the lunchtime soup on.

Babychino was a boy calf, lively and

curious. He had a nap and then he got up on his wobbly legs and looked for something to do. His friends Cocoa and Hazelnut were still asleep so he went to the barn door and pushed his nose around the edge; the door opened a bit more. In a flash he was outside and in the windy yard. The cobbles felt funny on his tiny feet. Which way should he go? A loud noise frightened him:

"Cock a doodle doo!" The fierce black cockerel crowed proudly. "You'll get into trouble!"

Babychino ran across the yard, round the corner and into a green field. The gate was open and a worn brown path led far away. Where did it go?

By now Cosmo had reached Goodly Harbour and was sitting with his cousin sipping coffee and trying the new Christmas cake ice cream.

"Mmm, nice and spicy, creamy too. Just a hint more cinnamon, cousin," said Cosmo. "It's very good."

"Try this one," urged Mr Rocadello, and he pushed a pale pink dish towards him.

Cosmo dug his spoon into it. 'Rose and Pomegranate', said the label. He rolled it around his mouth and it smelled sweetly.

"Ah! That's very gentle and perfumed, perhaps for the ladies?"

"Yes, yes just what I thought! A lighter flavour for after dinner."

Cosmo looked at his watch. Must be going soon, he told himself.

"Could I take a little sample for Maria? I think she would love this one."

"Of course, try the last one, please." It was pale green; he took a spoonful. Mr Rocadello sat forward, arms on the table.

"Got it?" he frowned.

No answer.

"Pear?" Cosmo asked hopefully.

"No."

Cosmo looked through the window where he could see some empty crates piled up outside. Each one had a paper picture stuck onto one end.

"Grape?"

Mr Rocadello was very relieved. "What do you think of it?"

Cosmo didn't want to say the wrong thing.

"It's nice but… but… not a very forceful flavour. Why don't you mix it with something else?"

His cousin was quiet, he knew Cosmo was right.

"What about a little grated cheese?" said Cosmo. "People end a meal with cheese and grapes, don't they?"

Mr Rocadello frowned. Preposterous! *And yet?* He sat thinking.

Cosmo didn't dare to get up and go. Then a big smile spread over his cousin's face.

"I'll try a test batch now. Just wait a minute." And he disappeared into the cold dairy, talking to himself. "Soft quiet base, maybe a hint of cream, hint of lemon?"

Cosmo knew he definitely should be going and was feeling anxious now. Lunch would be ready and he had endless chores to do. He tapped his fingers impatiently on the table, "Do hurry up cousin!"

Back at the farm, Maria put the large black pot on top of the stove. The vet was coming later on to check all the calves. She just had to collect the eggs and by the time she had put the elastic bands on the Bilberry Farm egg boxes, another hour had passed.

Cosmo wasn't back yet. She could hear one of the cows mooing, and knew very well it was Toffee Nose so she went to the barn to see what was the matter. Toffee Nose was making a strange noise; a worried noise. There was no sign of Babychino. Maria raced around frantically searching for him but he wasn't to be found. She put her arms around the distressed cow's neck and hugged her.

"Don't worry little Mama, I'll find him!"

Then she realised that she had not opened the latch on the barn door when she came in; it was already open. Babychino had got out. She went cold.

"He's got out into the farm!"

Maria was a bit frightened and tried to imagine where a small calf who had never been outside in the rest of the world, would go? Everything would be new and different, and… dangerous. She shuddered. The main road, the vet's car, the tractors, the stream, the cliffs, the lake! Oh no, not the lake!

She gathered speed and ran down the brown track worn in the grassy field, to the edge of the cliff with its dry scratchy bushes; a small coffee-coloured tuft of hair was stuck to one of them. Fear crept over her.

A rocky hill lead sharply down to the steep craggy cliffs. She could hear Babychino. Without a thought, she scrambled down the steep slope as far as she could and saw him, shivering and crying on a narrow flat edge. He couldn't go any further and was very frightened.

"I'm coming! I'm coming little one! Don't cry!" she called.

She got down on her hands and knees, hanging onto the odd grassy tufts, and climbing down, down, down, she stretched out sideways to try and reach him. Catching hold of his leg, she pulled him towards her and finally hugged him close.

"You're safe now, I've got you! I've got you!"

Maria's troubles were only just beginning. How was she to get back up the dangerous rocky cliff with a tired calf to carry?

# Chapter 5

# The Cliff rescue

Cosmo drove his van home very fast indeed. He knew he was late and Maria would be cross with him. He collected the straw bales first from the store in the far field and when he got to the farmyard it seemed unusually quiet. He went inside; Maria wasn't there but the soup was bubbling on the stove; in fact the soup had nearly boiled away, which seemed a little strange.

Cosmo had a funny feeling. He called Maria's name several times. There was no answer. He searched in the cheese barn, the chicken house, the pig pen, the vegetable garden and the orchard. He ran to the cow shed where the calves all stood looking at him.

Toffee Nose gave a mournful "moo!" No Babychino stood beside her. Cosmo was very worried now. Something told him to go to the lake to look for his wife and calf.

He too followed the brown path worn across the grassy field, until the grass ran out. Then the hillside dropped away to steep sheer rocks and puddles trapped in deep clefts. How could a little calf get down here?

He crouched, holding onto the rocks to help him climb down. Looking around frantically, the wind blowing in his face, he saw something he didn't want to believe – Maria and Babychino huddled together on the farthest ledge, cold and afraid. How had she got that far down?

"Maria! Maria! I can't reach you! What shall I do? I don't want you to fall into the lake!" He fell onto his knees, then he stretched out his arms in desperation but he couldn't reach them.

"I'm alright Cosmo, don't come any nearer," Maria told him calmly. "I am wedged in here tightly and Babychino is asleep. Go home and telephone for help, there's a dear," and she smiled bravely at him. "He's in such a state he might fall over the edge," she told herself.

"I don't want to leave you," called Cosmo, almost hysterical.

"I know dear, but you must. Go and get help *now*!" she insisted, nodding to make him understand.

Cosmo turned away, bitterly unhappy that he could not rescue his dear little wife. If only his cousin hadn't kept him eating ice cream. He climbed up the ridge onto the rocks, then reached the grass and ran like a madman, arms and legs flying round and round until he got to the farm, breathless and panting. He grabbed the phone and rang 777 for the police.

Sgt Huff answered quickly in his office.

"Sergeant, it's Cosmo from Bilberry Farm, my wife and a calf are stuck on a ledge on the cliffs. Can you send somebody to rescue her at once? Please hurry, it's getting so windy on the lake now and I am so afraid of them falling!" He stifled his sobs and bit his finger to stop himself crying.

"Now Cosmo, don't you worry. Say calm. I need some more details from you. Where exactly on the cliff are they?"

"Between Higher Rushing and the first woods farther down the lake, that's where my land goes over the edge."

"No landing place there, then?"

"No, sergeant, the cliffs are sheer."

"Any access from the top?"

"Well, I couldn't reach her, it's too narrow for a grown man."

"Anyway, don't trouble yourself Cosmo, leave it all to me," said Sgt Huff kindly, sensing his panic. "Have you got any lights you could rig up just to mark the location for us?"

"Yes, I could run the Land Rover over there and put the lights on."

"Good, that would be very helpful. You

do that and I'll get on to it straight away. Off you go, we'll be there soon, I promise."

Sgt Huff put the phone down. This was going to be a problem. There was no helicopter in their part of the country. The harbour launch could go, and possibly Jack could to do it? How would they get up the cliff as it was so steep? Could they possibly reach them from the top of the cliff?

He rang Captain Lively at the harbour office. Jack answered the phone.

"Goodly Harbour office, Jack speaking."

"Hi Jack, is Lucas there?"

"No, sorry, sergeant, he's at a school meeting in Little Rushing today. Can I help?"

"Well, I've got a big problem. Maria and a baby calf are stuck on the cliff edge below Bilberry Farm. We've got to rescue them somehow."

"I'll get the launch out sir, at once. Pick you up straight away on the pontoon, bye."

Jack rang Mr Noodlenutt straight away.

"Have you got a ladder on your crocodile vehicle?"

"Yes, Jack."

"Does it extend?"

"Yes, Jack."

"Are you busy right now?"

"No, Jack."

"Then can you help me with a cliff rescue?"

"Certainly, why didn't you say? What's up?"

"Maria and a baby calf are stuck on the cliffs just below Bilberry Farm."

"You'll need a sling for the calf, Jack, to stop it struggling. Got one?"

"No, sir."

"Leave it to me."

"Meet you by the pontoon in front of the police station. 'Bye." And Jack was gone.

Mr Noodlenutt thought quickly. One of the sandbags from the builders should do it, he had one with wood in it. They'd need a rope, too. Quickly he grabbed all the things and a woolly blanket. He filled Crocco with two bottles of green lemonade and kept one for a spare. Then he opened the garage door and was off. Down the slipway they went, bobbing into the water. He revved the engine and they were at the pontoon in seconds.

Sgt Huff got his climbing boots and

ropes, shouted out the news to Mrs Huff, and told her she was in charge of the telephone for the next hour or two. He left his office and crossed the road to the waterside where Jack was waiting in the harbour launch. He climbed aboard. He didn't know Mr Noodlenutt was following them, or about Jack organising the important ladder.

"Afternoon Jack, this is a bit of a to-do, isn't it?"

"Yes," agreed the young harbour officer, who had already put the kettle on, charged up his ship-to-shore radio, phoned the doctor to stand by, and sent Mr Rocadello to be with his cousin to keep him calm.

Mr Noodlenutt followed the launch up the lake some distance behind. He had some marvellous gadgets in Crocco's cockpit and hoped that some of them might be useful. It had turned into a cloudy, windy autumn day and there was no doubt it must be cold out on that rocky ledge where Maria and Babychino were sitting.

The little calf had a furry coat and he

kept Maria warm. She had run out of the house in just her skirt and cardigan and her small farm boots but she did have her warm, blue woolly socks on that Auntie Bessie always knitted her for Christmas. She tried not to look down; it was a long way to the rippling water and it made her feel a bit dizzy.

At Bilberry Farm, the vet and Mr Rocadello had both arrived to help poor Cosmo out. Mr Rocadello was very sorry he had kept Cosmo so long at the ice cream parlour.

"I did bring you some ice cream that you thought Maria might like, I have it in my van for you," he said kindly, but Cosmo really didn't care.

"Come and help me with the calves," suggested Ronald Jolly, the vet. "It will take your mind off things."

"I must put my Land Rover on the clifftop first," insisted Cosmo. "I told Sgt Huff I would."

"Alright, let's do that," agreed Ron. So the old grey Land Rover was placed safely a little way back from the edge and Cosmo fixed up a generator with an extra light. He didn't want a flat battery as well.

"Now," said Ron, "I think you should milk the little calf's mother. She will have too much milk today and will be getting very full up."

"Oh yes, I hadn't thought of that," replied Cosmo, and they spent some time in the barn with the cows and the calves, keeping busy until all the animals were fed and had clean straw.

Mr Rocadello spent his time in the kitchen. He made tea for them and rescued Maria's soup from burning. He cooked a lasagne and a chocolate cake and kept very busy too. The cuckoo clock in the kitchen cuckooed three times but nobody brought Maria back.

Cosmo went backwards and forwards to the Land Rover on the clifftop. He tried to lower a blanket and some soup to Maria but it kept going past her, and Maria didn't want to stretch out in case she missed it and fell off the ledge. Cosmo felt utterly helpless; he had done everything he could. The three men went together and sat in the vehicle on the clifftop, staring down at the lake, watching and waiting. At last the launch arrived.

Spotting the light with his binoculars, Sgt Huff directed Jack to the foot of the cliffs and they could all clearly see Maria in her red cardigan high above them. Then the chug, chug, chugging of another engine could be heard and Sgt Huff turned to see Crocco's glass bubble approaching.

"What's he doing here?" he said angrily. "He's always sticking his nose into everything. This is professional work, a co-ordinated rescue," he told Jack.

"Yes, but we need him," said Jack quietly.

"Need him? Indeed we do not, Jack! We are trained for such events, we will keep calm and work out a plan. Why we have a plan already, don't we? We have everything we need without that crank Noodlenutt's advice or his stupid vehicle!"

"Do we, sir?"

"Yes, yes! Of course we do, Jack. Trust me, boy. I am your superior so you just listen to me. I shall climb up the cliff and rescue them both. I'm quite a skilled climber, you know."

"You don't need to do that sir, Mr Noodlenutt has a large extending ladder in his car."

"What?" exclaimed Sgt Huff.

"Yes, I telephoned him and he offered to help. It really would be much easier, sir."

Sgt Huff was silenced. How did that idiot Noodlenutt always manage it? He seemed to be able to do anything and everything.

Crocco nudged into place beside *Lionheart* the harbour launch. The bubble opened and Mr Noodlenutt's head popped out.

"Ready, Sgt Huff? Jack?"

He pressed a button in the cockpit and up slid the ladder. It had three sections all connected inside each other. The ladder went up and up and up until it was 60 feet high. It would reach Maria easily.

"Here's the sling."

And Mr Noodlenutt unfolded the rather dirty bag with the big straps and handed it to Jack.

"I think I'll go up, sir, if it's alright with you. I'm a bit smaller and maybe a bit lighter. You can follow me if you like, a bit of stability at the bottom, do you think?"

"You're probably right, go ahead," the policeman told him begrudgingly. "I'll follow. You stay here, Noodlenutt."

Maria could see what was going on. Cosmo lay on the rocks on his tummy, calling to her.

"I can see them, my dear! They are coming for you! Hold on!"

Jack fearlessly scrambled up the strong, thin ladder. He could see it would be alright. It was a bit gusty up there and swayed just a little but he had taken a boat hook with him. When he was alongside Maria he held the bag out to her on the hook.

"Maria! So glad you are alright! Now, if you could slip this bag around the calf it would be a great help. Can you?"

She smiled and nodded then slowly she put the woven bag around the calf; he fitted into it easily.

"Now pass him by the straps. Don't lean out in case the weight of the bag pulls you over. I'll fit the boathook into the loops to help to take the weight. We don't want the little fellow to struggle, do we?"

Slowly, gradually, Babychino was lowered into the grasp of Jack. He carefully went backwards down the ladder and passed the bag to Sgt Huff.

"Got him, Jack! Well done! Coming down, Noodlenutt, out of the way!" and Sgt Huff stumbled onto the roof light and then onto *Lionheart* where he lost his balance, and he and the calf ended up in a tangle on the deck of the launch. Babychino squealed loudly. Mr Noodlenutt leapt onto the deck with a rope and deftly tied Babychino firmly to a seat. Sgt Huff got himself up, dusted down his uniform, glared at Mr Noodlenutt and went back up the ladder to help Jack.

Jack was already hand-in-hand with Maria; he had slipped a self-inflating life jacket over her head, secured her to a clip around his waist and was quietly and gently coaxing her downwards, guiding her feet, until Sgt Huff could reach one of her hands, and then he carried her into *Lionheart*. This time he did not fall over.

Up above, Cosmo, Mr Rocadello and Ron cheered.

"Well done! Well done!" and Cosmo blew her a kiss.

Maria waved back, smiling.

Mr Noodlenutt pressed the button and the ladder retracted, folding itself neatly into the cockpit interior. Maria was wrapped in the bright checked blanket and given a cup of hot, sweet tea. Jack had managed everything splendidly, with no fuss at all.

"Thank you, Mr Noodlenutt. Without the ladder it wouldn't have been possible," said Jack nicely.

"Thank you, everybody," said Maria, and Babychino mooed. She sat beside him on the floor and stroked him.

"You're a bad little boy," she scolded. "Look at all this trouble you've caused." Then she smiled her most brilliant smile at the men who were watching her. "You must all come back to the farm for supper, I insist. Cosmo will want to thank you himself. He could pick me up at the Forest Jetty? What do you think?"

"I must radio some calls in first," said Jack. "Then I could come to supper. Thank you, Maria."

"I would be honoured to dine with you and Cosmo," and Mr Noodlenutt bowed.

"I am the only policeman in Goodly Harbour and I cannot leave my office for too long. I need to return soon, so Maria, I am sorry but I cannot come to supper."

He did not even smile or thank her.

"I will take *Lionheart* back for you, Jack, if you are not going to return," he offered in a slightly sniffy way.

"That's very kind of you sir, I'm sure Captain Lively will give his permission."

Jack radioed the harbour office, the hospital and Bilberry Farm. Everybody involved in the rescue was to stand down. Jack could write up his report tomorrow; he logged the time, recorded the mileage on *Lionheart*, got Sgt Huff to sign for the launch and handed him the keys.

"I must say, Mr Noodlenutt, I am really looking forward to a ride in your wonderful car – Crocco isn't it?" and Crocco flashed his lights at Jack's mention of his name.

"We can swap the passengers over at Forest Jetty," Sgt Huff told them, and left at once, motoring down the lake to where Cosmo would be waiting for them.

Jack climbed into Crocco who submerged quickly and Mr Noodlenutt began to show him everything. Being underneath the lake was a totally new experience which Jack thoroughly enjoyed. He soon understood the controls and marvelled at how it all worked, especially the green lemonade. He didn't want to arrive at the jetty too soon, so that Sgt Huff got some of the praise for the rescue.

By the time Crocco surfaced at Forest Jetty, Cosmo, Maria and Babychino had been reunited. Tears of joy had been shed and Sgt Huff was hugged and thanked by Cosmo, Mr Rocadello and Ron Jolly. He wriggled away uncomfortably.

"Just doing my job," he mumbled,

straightening his uniform. "Glad everyone's safe," and he escaped back to *Lionheart* intent on returning to his office to make his official report.

Crocco drove out of the lake and onto the gravelly beach, following the Land Rover up the hill and off to Bilberry Farm a few miles away.

Sgt Huff stood on the deck and watched them go; he was still a little cross that Mr Noodlenutt had been asked to help, and yet, as they disappeared, he felt lonely and left out.

"It might have been rather nice to have supper at Bilberry Farm; there might have been some of Mr Rocodello's ice cream and some of Maria's famous cheese and Cosmo's ham." Yes, he was rather sorry he had refused now. "Never mind, Mrs Huff will be waiting for me. Maybe it will be lamb chops with mint and onion gravy for supper tonight." And he cheered himself up. What a lot he had to write up in his white notebook! He patted the notebook in his pocket. In fact he ought to jot down a few points now, just so that he didn't forget.

He pulled out the white notebook with

the pencil attached to it but the string became entangled in the keys which were also in his pocket and they all came out at once. The keys did a perfect somersault and Sgt Huff watched in horror as they turned over and over beyond his reach and plopped into the lake with a splash. He watched the rippling circles spreading out where the keys had hit the water.

"Oh no, they've gone!"

There was a spare set in the harbour office. He didn't want to ring Lucas Lively to tell him how stupid he had been. He paced the small deck, biting his nails. What was he going to do? He kept looking over the side in case by magic the keys somehow would float to the surface; but they did not, nor were they likely to. They were very firmly embedded in the bottom of the lake by now.

Sgt Huff stared into the distance. He knew he couldn't get them by himself, the lake was too deep. There was only one person who could get those keys back for him. He didn't even want to breathe his name. It was so annoying; poor Sgt Huff felt very unhappy trying to decide what was his duty as a policeman and what he actually wanted to do. He did not want to ask Mr Noodlenutt for anything but, what else could he do? Could Col Boodle-Smith help him out? He could signal to him quite easily with his torch… but what could that old buffoon really do that would solve the problem? The answers were all the same – nothing. Nothing for it but to swallow his pride and ring Bilberry Farm on the ship-to-shore radio. Mr Noodlenutt was the only person in the whole world who could get those keys back.

Unhappily, he heaved a big sigh and switched on the radio. He dialled up the number and it was some time before it was answered. Cosmo said the number.

"Good evening Cosmo, Sgt Huff here, everything alright?"

"Oh yes, Sgt, so nice of you to ring us, Maria is fine and all is well. Thank you! Thank you!"

Sgt Huff cleared his throat and coughed.

"Well, the thing is, Cosmo, could I have a word with Jack? Just a bit of official business, you know."

"Of course, he's right here."

"Jack Dooit speaking."

"Ah Jack. I've hit a bit of a problem, well it's about the launch actually, I… I… He couldn't seem to say it.

"Yes, sergeant? What's happened?" Jack asked quietly, sensing his difficulty. "Can I help at all?"

"Yes, you can. I seem to have lost the keys."

"Oh… Any idea where?"

"Eh, eh, yes. They are in the lake, probably at the bottom by now. I'm afraid I dropped them overboard."

There was a short silence.

"Never mind, it happens all the time on the lake. You wouldn't believe how often. We'll be with you in a couple of ticks, don't you worry. See you soon. 'Bye."

And it was all over. Sgt Huff sat down. He wasn't used to asking anyone for help. He felt very stupid, in fact he felt like crying.

Not long afterwards, Jack appeared in the farm Land Rover by himself. Sgt Huff was puzzled. Jack jumped out, smiling.

"You've to come and eat first. We'll sort

the keys out later. Come on, Maria's dishing up a smashing feast. You don't want to miss it!"

Sgt Huff had no choice but to get in the Land Rover with Jack.

"Oh, and Maria phoned Mrs Huff. She's going to visit her sister Freda and had left you a salad. She's switched the phone over to head office for the evening so everything is sorted." He beamed a big smile at the surprised policeman. Sgt Huff wasn't pleased.

When they reached the farm, the fire was blazing and the lights were all on. Cosmo had finished milking, with his cousin and Ron's help. The table was laid with a red-and-white checked cloth and there were several bottles of wine open.

"Come and sit down, sergeant," invited Cosmo. "Now, what is your first name? We none of us know it, you must have one. Tell us please."

Sgt Huff looked embarrassed.

"I don't use it much, it's a bit of a mouthful. My mother… you see was very keen on Shakespeare."

"Well, you can tell us surely!" smiled Jack.

"It's… um…, Othello."

"Oh," said everyone together, and shut up.

"Just call me Huff, eh? I think it suits me better." And Sgt Huff actually smiled, and really he looked very nice when he smiled.

The food was a proper banquet. Big bowls of steaming vegetable broth with cheese croutons, lasagne and salad, and warm crusty bread and butter, chocolate cake, rose and pomegranate ice cream, Christmas cake ice cream, and grape and cheese ice cream, with wine and coffee. There was laughter and chatter, and lots of warm happiness swirled around the room and some of it curled around Sgt Huff and he began to smile a lot. He was really enjoying himself.

"This ice cream is rather good," he told Mr Rocadello. "Unusual, but I like it."

"Good! That's very good! Thank you. It's Maria's cheese that is in this recipe."

"Well don't get too carried away or you'll be putting Cosmo's ham in it next!" joked Sgt Huff.

For a special treat, Maria opened a box of Mrs Magill's nice but naughty soft nougat. Each piece glistened with a slice of cherry surrounded by chips of delicious nuts, and sat in a white paper ruffle.

"Mmm, these are one of my favourites," Jack told her as he closed his eyes and chewed the honeyed sweet.

Everyone took a piece. Mr Noodlenutt was rather quiet as he ate his nougat. He was trying to think of the best way to find and recover the keys. Keys were funny things; they never seemed to be found anywhere near where they fell in. Crocco's metal detector seemed the best way. It could sweep the lake floor easily. The trouble was it would pick up anything that was metal, not just the keys. However, it was a start. He would have to go down in his diving suit and oversee the operation. It was going to be a late night.

As all the men chewed on their nougat, each one was thinking hard about how the task ahead should be approached. Good teamwork must come first at all times and their differences must be put aside, for tonight anyway. Mrs Magill's nougat seemed to work its own sort of magic.

# Chapter 6

# Treasure hunting

As soon as supper was over, the serious work began. They wished everybody goodnight and Jack, Sgt Huff and Mr Noodlenutt climbed into Crocco. Sgt Huff sat very silently in the back seats. Jack was allowed to drive and Crocco entered the lake at the Forest Jetty. It was very dark and the trees waved and cast shadows, owls hooted and a fox barked.

"Press that blue button, Jack." And from under the submersible car came a metal-detecting head.

"Now the orange button, Jack," and a round light switched on underneath.

"Steady now, hover Crocco and turn the headlights off," instructed Mr Noodlenutt. He stepped into his canvas suit and pulled himself into the rubber arms and neck. Jack helped him as he wriggled and jiggled it on. Then he lifted the big copper diving helmet and placed it carefully on the curly head, finishing with a pair of gloves and a net bag. Sgt Huff watched everything; he was truly amazed; he had never seen anything like it in his life. Jack seemed quite at home. He was a very quick learner, trying hard to make sense of it all and to understand what Mr Noodlenutt was going to do.

"Just open another bottle of lemonade will you, Jack, before I go out? There's a black rubber cap marked FUEL so pour it in there, would you?"

Jack quickly obeyed.

Sgt Huff couldn't believe his eyes. Green lemonade in a car?

When Mr Noodlenutt was ready he opened the door in the floor, climbed down into the space, closed the door and pressurised the small compartment. Carefully and slowly he stepped into his big diving boots, strapped them up, and when the pressure was the same as the water pressure outside, the door opened on its hinges. He made his way out into the dark waters of the lake. Lots of fish and eels were darting about, attracted by the bright circle of light.

The tube in the top of the copper diving helmet was attached to another tube inside the car and air was fed to him constantly by a pump. It was possible to talk to Crocco and Jack through the helmet's intercom system. The metal detector had an electro-magnet around the rim and on Mr Noodlenutt's signal, Jack was to turn it on. This was a silver button with a dial indicating the strength of the magnetic force applied. It was used with a fine probe which could dig into the silt and stones on the lake floor.

"Switch on!"

Jack turned the dial and the needle swung into the middle with a buzzing sound. Around the circle of light the metal detector swept and beeped loudly. Holding the probe, a swirl of mud floated around Mr Noodlenutt. With a sucking noise, a metal object was pulled towards the strong magnet and landed with a clang.

"Just an old hinge," came Mr Noodlenutt's voice. One old key, some rusty nails, a tin, and an old hammer were next.

"Move along a bit, Crocco," and the crocodile car obeyed. More mud and silt and metal rubbish. The beeping got very loud and the probe uncovered something quite large. After a bit of digging around, a small carved figure appeared, very muddy and dirty. It too went into the bag to be examined later.

"Move along, Crocco!" Sgt Huff and Jack looked at each other and then at their watches. It was getting late. How long should they go on trying for? It was up to the boss.

"We'll get them soon, I'm sure," said Jack. Sgt Huff nodded glumly and said nothing. A new circle of light was uncovered and the button beeped loudly again. Under the probe, glinting in the light, lay the keys, which jumped out and leapt onto the magnet!

"Bingo! Got them!"

Also uncovered was a ring, more tins and a pair of scissors. Mr Noodlenutt put the ring and the keys into the bag.

"Good, we can all go home now. Switch off blue, orange and silver, Jack."

Mr Noodlenutt walked clumsily back in his large lead boots to the hatch with the net bag containing its interesting finds.

Sgt Huff smiled at last. "I'm so glad," he said. "Thank goodness for that."

He waited until Mr Noodlenutt had got back inside again and then he thanked him as nicely as it was possible for Sgt Huff.

"Very grateful, Noodlenutt, good effort. Thank you."

"No need to tell Captain Lively… is there, sir?" asked Jack.

"Well, it was just a little treasure hunting as you might say, wasn't it? After all, we've found some treasure!"

Sgt Huff actually helped Mr Noodlenutt out of his canvas suit.

"This has been a very interesting experience," he told the old diver carefully.

"Good! Good!" Glad you came along Huff, dear fellow," replied Mr Noodlenutt cheerfully. "Now, who's driving old *Lionheart* back to Goodly Harbour?"

"I will, sir," replied Jack quickly, "Sgt Huff would probably like a turn to drive Crocco!"

At this the policeman paled, and stuttered, "Oh, er, no, I don't think so, I have to—"

"Nonsense! Crocco does most of the work, you just help him to steer. Why don't you try it?"

So they turned back to Forest Jetty, where it was cold and dark. Jack jumped out with the now famous keys and onto *Lionheart*.

"Poor old boat, left here on your own, we're off home now. Let's go." And he turned the key and *Lionheart* sprang into life. He led the way down the lake with Crocco following, and it wasn't long until the lights of Goodly

Harbour came into sight. Sgt Huff had enjoyed himself so much he was almost sorry to be back.

It was very late; the clock tower, watching the two boats glide in, struck a quarter to eleven. He could relax, now everyone was safely home. The streets were empty, all was quiet and the three men went home to bed.

Crocco was feeling extra tired and Mr Noodlenutt put a large sheet over the bonnet when they were finally back in Eight Bells Cottage. He went into his workshop and laid the items he had found on the bench on a cloth. He knew that sometimes things that have been under the water for a long time started to crack as they dried out. He looked at them carefully and then got some soapy water and a small brush and cleaned them gently.

The ring was a large gold one with a square top; in the square was a coat of arms with a lion cut into it. It was quite heavy and when it was washed it was bright and shiny, and Mr Noodlenutt was delighted with it. He had seen the coat of arms before, on the flag flying over Goodly Harbour town hall. The ring must have belonged to somebody important. As for the statue, it was silver in colour and was a lady holding a baby; it was also very beautiful when it was cleaned up. Sometimes these statues came from churches and people often had them in their homes. It could have come from anywhere.

Leaving them on his bench to dry, Mr Noodlenutt yawned and knew it was really time for bed. He didn't go to smoke his pipe on the quayside as usual, he was just too tired.

Sgt Huff found his wife in bed fast asleep and he didn't even bother to write his notebook up, for the first time ever. He lay awake in his bed listening to the clock striking twelve and smiled to himself.

"That Noodlenutt's not a bad fellow really," he said out loud.

"What did you say, Otto?" asked Mrs Huff, half asleep.

"Nothing Nora, go back to sleep." And Sgt Huff closed his eyes. What a day!

But that is not the end of the story, because Mr Noodlenutt found out that the ring had belonged to the baron who had founded the town, Baron Augustus Neville-de-Lyon, and it is now displayed in a glass case in the museum. Sgt Huff and Jack were very proud indeed. The little silver statue had been stolen from the church many years before with some precious goblets and plates and the church elders were delighted to have the Madonna of the Lake back. She was put in a special place where everyone could see her, high up on a stone niche in the wall. So, the long search for the keys had been very useful after all.

# ADVENTURE THREE

## Chapter 7

# The Serpent of the Lake

Now it's time to introduce you to some of the people who live on the other side of the lake, at Little Rushing on the Water. You have briefly met Dr Proctor, but not his two German sausage dogs, Pepperoni and Frankfurter, Peppi and Franki for short. They had been specially trained to collect the tickets and pull the train's whistle when required.

Both dogs wore navy blue peaked caps with GHRC embroidered on the front in gold. I expect you have worked out this means Goodly Harbour Railway Company, and Peppi and Franki went on every journey that Dr Proctor made. The three of them lived at Little Rushing above the railway sheds where *Trooper* the engine and the two carriages were kept. From their round attic window there was a magnificent view up the railway line and over the whole lake.

The sheds had plenty of storage for all the things Dr Proctor collected for his inventions, mostly things that other people threw away: old wheels, springs, nuts and bolts, pots and pans, string, wire; almost anything found a new home. All the *really* useful things that Dr Proctor might need were tied into the cab of the engine and rattled and clanged as *Trooper* crossed the bridge.

The ticket office at the station was run by Mr and Mrs Glum, generally known as The Glums to the residents of the village. This couple were the most miserable people you are ever likely to meet during the whole of your lifetime. Mrs Glum was small with a pasty face, glasses and thin lank hair which she hardly ever washed, and she never, never smiled. Mr Glum was tall and thin with tufty hair and a big nose; he never smiled either. When the visitors arrived at Little Rushing they got off the bus and went into the station to buy a ticket for the train ride across the lake, or for the train and boat ride. So everybody that caught the train met the Glums, which was a great pity because there wasn't much of a welcome for anyone.

Now you can see how nice it was for all the visitors to be greeted by two very friendly sausage dogs who took your tickets and were extremely pleased to see you. Dr Proctor wandered through the train saying hello to the children before the journey and making sure everyone was comfortable. Then one of the dogs would pull the steam whistle, the engine started and off *Trooper* went. When he got up to top speed, everything rattled and swayed as they crossed the bridge that spanned the lake to get to the other side at Goodly Harbour. It was such a pretty place, with its pavement cafes and well-kept houses with their red geraniums outside, that all the passengers wanted to get out and enjoy themselves.

There were boat rides up the lake run by twin brothers Jago and Jebs Mulligan, who both had red hair and large bushy beards. They lived together in Little Rushing in the first cottage past the station. Each day they made the trip up and down the lake several times and waved to each other as they passed by, one in a red boat and one in a blue boat. In the summer they were very busy indeed but they never got tired of driving their boats, or of telling the visitors rather questionable stories about the lake and its history. They would have liked something really exciting to tell their passengers, and one year there was.

During the winter, a huge pine branch broke off a big old tree. It was a most unusual twisted shape with an arch in the middle, and where it had sheared off from the trunk of the tree there was a large jagged split down the middle. The other end was blunt with several rotten branches sticking out. The heavy rain and strong winds of the winter storms pushed the log up to the top end of the lake near the waterfall, where it rolled and bumped along in the rough water, finally wedging itself under an overhanging branch and tangled weeds. It lay still for a long time, just rotting. The lake froze over and covered it up; nobody knew it was there.

When the ice and the mountain snows melted in the spring the lake was very full and the log became free and floated down the lake. As soon as spring came, Jebs and Jago painted their boats, varnished the woodwork, polished the chrome handles, replaced the ropes and anchors, and waited for some early visitors. When the sun came out and people wanted to go on the first boat trip of the season, Jebs spotted the log floating in the edge. Logs could be dangerous. Sometime later, Jago also saw it but the current in the water and the wake of the boats had turned the log over and the rounded end showed above the water. The log turned hither and thither, over and over, occasionally becoming caught in the weeds and debris by the banks of the lake. Every time it came to rest, a different part of it appeared above the water; it looked like something very strange with a head, a tail and a humped back, rather like the famous Loch Ness monster!

Jebs and Jago laughed together about the 'serpent in the lake' they had seen. During that spring they only glimpsed it twice, because the log disappeared for a while when it tangled up and was held fast under the surface. After a particularly heavy storm the log was set free from its prison to float around the lake. It turned itself around and came to rest beside the motor launch of Col Boodle-Smith. He woke up from his morning nap while on *Duty* to see a humped back shape, gnarled and warty, floating by. The split and twisted end came past the window and slowly disappeared.

"Oh, er! What was that?" thought the sleepy colonel, who was only half awake. "Must be dreaming. Looked like a large snake."

He closed his eyes again, back into a warm, dreamy doze. By the time he had come to and collected his thoughts, the log was long gone.

Eagle-eyed Sgt Huff saw something on the lake while doing his observations one evening. The next day, he alerted Col Boodle-Smith with his usual signal at 10.30 a.m.:

*BE ALERT. POSSIBLE*
*DANGER TO SHIPPING.*
*OBJECT FLOATING IN*
*LAKE.*

When he received the message, Col Boodle-Smith's memory was jogged, and he replied:

*WILL DO. ON THE CASE.*

He scanned the lake constantly after the message, wondering about the snake he had seen, but he put it down to the sloe gin making him dream.

Jebs and Jago still laughed about the serpent in the lake, which they had only seen twice. The first time the rounded end was showing and it looked like a head, the other time the split end showed looking like a tail, and they thought it a huge joke to tell their passengers about 'the serpent of the lake'. It was rather strange how similar the lump of wood looked to the Loch Ness monster, depending on how it rolled, with its sort of head, the twist in the body and the split in the tail; it was a very weird coincidence.

They mentioned it to the Glums in the ticket office, which was quite naughty of them, because they only really wanted to frighten Mrs Glum, but Mrs Glum wasn't frightened. Quite the opposite; her eyes gleamed and she told Mr Glum the news. All they could think of was the money that could be made. They decided at once to add this to their poster to try and attract more people on the boat trips, and had some red stickers made to put on their advertising boards, which said:

*Catch a glimpse of the Sea Serpent! Will you be lucky today?*

After this idea, Mr and Mrs Glum cheered up a bit, even smiling at one or two people.

As the summer progressed, the lake got quite busy and news of the serpent reached Captain Lucas Lively, the harbour master, who was rather annoyed he knew nothing about it. He asked Jebs and Jago Mulligan to come and see him.

"What's all this about, boys?"

The brothers looked at each other sheepishly.

"Well, captain, we've seen it a couple of times – just a hump in the water, probably nothing. The passengers like to hear our stories, you know what they're like: pirates and sea monsters, smugglers and shipwrecks, they love all that seaside folklore." They tried to make little of it. "Just a bit of fun, you know, captain."

"Do you think I should investigate it? Can you give me an exact location?" Captain Lively asked.

"Well no, not exactly," replied Jebs.

"You see, it's not in the same place twice," explained Jago.

"I tell you what, I'll get Jack to have a look. He'll do it," agreed Lucas quickly.

"Okay, captain. Fine by us," they chimed together, and got out of the office as fast as they could. What had started out as a bit of a joke was now turning into something else. However, business is business.

Jack was then duly told by Captain Lively to investigate the sightings. He took *Lionheart* the harbour launch up the lake to check it out. However, the very day that Jack went to look, there had been some heavy rainfall and the log was lying below some trees, hidden at the edge. It was impossible to see anything other than an old piece of wood half-submerged. Nothing that remotely resembled a serpent or a sea monster broke the surface that day. Jack was disappointed; he had been looking forward to lots of excitement and was equipped with his camera and binoculars to record his momentous findings. He had been so hoping to find the sea serpent. Coming back down the lake he passed *Duty* moored on the pontoon outside Col Boodle-Smith's garden.

The colonel was sipping his coffee on the aft deck.

"Ahoy there, Jack lad!" he called to the launch. Jack slowed down and stopped for a chat. He told the colonel all about the sightings of the sea serpent.

"Well, well I never!" blustered the old gentleman. "I think I saw it, you know. Came right alongside my vessel, probably smelt me. What a lucky escape I had! I could have been breakfast. Well, well, well, I shall have to keep a very close eye out now. Sergeant Huff saw it as well, I'm sure. We'll track it down, no place to hide now on our lake!" and he patted Jack on the back.

"Better luck next time eh, my boy? I'll give you a hand, don't you worry. Our very own Loch Ness monster, eh?"

Jack revved up *Lionheart* and proceeded back to report to the harbour master.

At Little Rushing ticket office, business was booming. The Glums, who were not so glum now, were advertising the sea serpent for all it was worth. Jebs and Jago had been very busy, with the blue and red boats full every day. People came with binoculars and cameras, jostling each other in excitement. The twins, of course, knew the serpent did not exist, and could not believe that an old lump of wood could cause such interest and extra money for everyone, so did not feel guilty. Well… only a little.

One afternoon, a mixture of strong winds and the wake from all the boats on the lake dislodged the huge branch. Its split trunk rolled upwards, and away it went floating down towards Goodly Harbour. Jebs skippering his red boat and Jago his blue boat both saw it, along with the fifty passengers they had on board between them. The tail fin was quite plain to see. By the time they motored nearer for a better look the branch had rolled to its twisted side and a hump appeared. The people watching gasped and were frightened; they begged the brothers to turn round in case the boats capsized. Lots of the passengers took photos, and now there was real evidence of 'the serpent in the lake'.

Then two teenage boys who had heard the news wanted to show off. They took a dingy with an outboard engine up the lake, looking for the serpent.

"We're not afraid!" they shouted out.

Finding the log, they circled it and then approached it at high speed. The log rolled in the disturbed water and the rounded end tipped up, looking just like a head rearing towards them. The terrified boys yelled and drove back, revving up to maximum speed, the boat bouncing wildly in the choppy water and the boys shouting, "It's going to attack us!"

The news spread like wildfire. When Dr Proctor heard about it he hurried off to see his old friend. He had hatched a plan to catch whatever it was and wanted to share his idea.

Mr Noodlenutt was not convinced. "Look here, Proctor," he said firmly. "There is no entry or exit into the lake. Nothing could possibly have grown in here, either."

"But how do you know there isn't an underground cavern leading from a river? I'd like to put some nets down across the lake and explore each section one at a time in Crocco. What about that?" Dr Proctor was very keen and nodded, trying to persuade him.

"I suppose it's worth a try." Mr Noodlenutt smiled, but said no more.

No plans were laid on that day. Dr Proctor had to wait patiently, however things took a turn in his favour. Once the news got out about the two boys and the sightings on the lake, suddenly Goodly Harbour and Little Rushing by the Water were in the news. The village became swamped in TV cameras, reporters and sightseers. Even a helicopter flew over several times a day, with a cameraman hanging precariously out of the doorway.

There was so much traffic that Sgt Huff had to dress Mrs Huff in his second-best uniform to control the cars engulfing the town. She greatly enjoyed it, stopping all the nosy parkers with her spotless white gloves. If anyone hooted impatiently, she ignored them and made them wait a little longer.

Mr Rocadello ran out of ice cream, and Maria had to come from the farm to help him serve in the shop. At Mrs Magill's cake shop, all carried on serenely, always an orderly queue outside, never running out of anything, everything replaced as always as if by magic.

The town clock had a lot to look at. It was very hard to watch over all the people; never had the town been so full.

Mr Noodlenutt didn't like the invasion of people. They sat on his slipway, peered into his windows, made a lot of noise at night and kept him awake.

Captain Lively had a phone call from the Minister for the Environment telling him that he was to use any means available to him to find and catch the sea serpent and hold it for inspection. A team of scientists from the Ministry would then be despatched to Goodly Harbour. It was an urgent and rather stern conversation. He was told to "get a move on with it". Lucas Lively quaked in his polished shoes.

"Yes sir, at once, sir," he promised, standing up to attention as he spoke. He called to Jack.

"Jack, Jack, in here at once!"

The young man rushed in straight away.

"Yes, Captain Lively?"

"We've got to sort this serpent thing out, Jack. Orders from the Ministry. How shall we do it"

Jack thought hard for a minute or two.

"I'll get Mr Noodlenutt and Dr Proctor here for a meeting at once."

"Good thinking. I'll ring them now." And Lucas got straight on the phone. Within the hour, the four men were sitting around a desk that was covered in maps and notebooks, pens and pencils. Coffee and cakes were specially sent by Mrs Magill, rather delicious chocolate twists with rosemary sprinkles.

"Leave it to us, Captain Lively," soothed Mr Noodlenutt, "we can do an underwater survey. We'll cover the grids we have marked on the map. It can't escape. Don't you worry, we shall find it. We'd like Jack to come with us and keep notes and man the underwater camera, is that okay?"

"Perfect."

Lucas felt better already.

"Radio me of any progress."

He relaxed at once. Jack would do it; he always did. He closed the door of his office. Peace and quiet at last.

"I'd like to talk to Jebs and Jago first,"

said Jack, as he bounded down the office stairs to the lake front. "I reckon they know more than anyone. They must have seen the thing, whatever it is."

"Send a message to them to meet us on the pontoon tomorrow morning before we set off," suggested Dr Proctor.

"Right, we'll go and get Crocco and all our equipment ready," said Mr Noodlenutt firmly. "So all meet on the pontoon at 8.00 a.m. tomorrow, there's only two days to go before the Fiesta and the town will be full to bursting. The fair and the fireworks bring so many visitors without all this serpent publicity as well."

I'll have to man *Trooper* on those days," fretted Dr Proctor, "that means we haven't got much time."

"See you tomorrow," smiled Jack, and left them both.

He had a few ideas of his own. He went off to see his mother, who lived next door to Jebs and Jago's Auntie Doris. Doris did the ironing for a lot of people and she knew everything that was going on. His mother opened the door and was delighted to see her son on the doorstep.

"Any tea, Ma?"

He kissed her on both cheeks and walked in.

"Yes love, Doris will be round in a minute, she always pops in at four o'clock for tea and we exchange news. You don't mind, do you?"

It was just what Jack wanted, tea and gossip.

"Of course not Ma, got any cake?"

With that, Auntie Doris appeared. She was everybody's auntie: small, round, tiny glasses perched on her nose, dimpled cheeks and a ready smile.

"Jack! Lovely to see you. You're such a busy young man now." And she kissed him heartily, and then produced a bunch of brightly coloured zinnias from behind her back.

"For you, Marguerita."

She offered them to Jack's mum. Very soon they were sitting with tea and almond cakes.

"Jebs and Jago alright?" asked Jack, munching hungrily.

"They're even busier than you!" laughed Doris. "This serpent thing has gone mad. Every day the boats are full, dawn to dusk, up and down the lake. They're not complaining mind you, but they're getting a bit tired of it. Lot of nonsense really, I'd say." Doris folded her arms and looked away with a strange suck of her teeth and a sigh.

"Oh really, know anything about it, Doris?" Jack tilted his head inquiringly.

"Well, I shouldn't say things really, but I've got an idea that serpent could be nothing more than an old tree trunk."

Jack stopped eating. She leaned forward and whispered.

"I hear things. It's quite possible it's as simple as that, just an old piece of rubbish that's been made into something by everyone. It's more than the joke it started out to be now, but how do we stop it? I dunno. Jebs and Jago will have to think of something quick. The whole place has gone mad. I don't like it, so there." And she pursed her lips and would say no more; in fact she looked quite upset.

"There there, Doris, now don't go upsetting yourself, maybe… Jack, could you have a quiet word with them? You know what I mean?"

His mother signalled to him with her eyes. He got the message.

"More tea, Doris? Those flowers are a sight for sore eyes, just lovely. My favourite." She beamed at her dearest friend. "More cake?"

Jack sat back thoughtfully. So that was it. Just a little bit of deception. Maybe it started as a joke, and look what's happened. Needs careful handling.

"Well Ma, Doris, that was a nice break. Got to get on now, thanks for the tea and cake. We'll sort it out, don't worry any more. See you soon. Enjoy the Fiesta and the fireworks."

And he kissed both of them goodbye. He had a lot to think about as he walked up the hill to the cottage Jebs and Jago shared. Sitting on an upturned wooden boat in their front garden, he wrote a short note to them and pushed it through their letter box. Then he went back to Goodly Harbour and sat quietly for a good long think to work out his plan.

# Chapter 8

# Blowing up things

When Jebs and Jago came home from work, weary and hungry, they found Jack's note.

"Looks like the game's up," the brothers decided. "Well, we've had some good business out of our serpent, can't argue with that. Got enough money for a new boat now. We're tired of it all anyway, so we'd better go and help Jack to catch this old monster, hadn't we?"

They were both on the pontoon at 8.00 a.m. sharp on the Goodly Harbour side of the lake. Jack greeted them coolly.

"Time to put an end to this now, boys," he told them. Both twins looked rather guilty.

"It just sort of grew," explained Jebs.

"We didn't set out to deliberately deceive people, it started as a joke really," continued Jago.

"Fair enough," said Jack, as Crocco cruised in beside them with Mr Noodlenutt and Dr Proctor looking out for them. The passengers climbed on board.

"Coo! Ain't this something!" chimed the brothers together, clutching each other's arms in alarm as the special car disappeared beneath the black water, with only the periscope visible on the surface.

The sonar screen glowed green and the echo pinged around them.

"Crocco will soon locate it," Mr Noodlenutt explained. "Jack, tell us the plan."

Jack smiled at them weakly, took a rather deep breath and proceeded with his very good plan.

"To save everyone's embarrassment, I think you should know we are setting out to blow up a large log."

Looks of astonishment met him.

"Yes, I'm afraid that's all it is, this terrifying monster from the deep, our so-called sea serpent. We should be glad really!" He laughed, hoping everyone else would see the joke. He continued swiftly before anyone could comment.

"At the finale of the Fiesta fireworks there is a loud burst of noise, hooting and cheering and clapping, so that is when the log will be blown up. A carefully controlled explosion set up by remote control will be carried out by Mr Noodlenutt, our explosives expert. There is no movement allowed on the lake because of the flypast, so no boats will be in danger for those five minutes. After all, it does present a danger to shipping and in our manual at the harbour office, I quote, 'it can be disposed of safely by any means appropriate'. We are going to lay the charges and set up the explosives now, once we have located our target. Does anyone know its last sighted position?"

But nobody did.

"Never mind," said Mr Noodlenutt, "Crocco will find it. Must be rather large and a very peculiar shape!"

Jack and Dr Proctor got together all the items they would need – detonators, cortex, explosive line and a timer. Jebs and Jago watched, goggle-eyed. Some minutes later, loud noises came from the sonar and a shape appeared on the screen.

"Got it!"

Crocco slowed down and steadily they located their target. The lights were switched on outside and Crocco halted.

"Does that look right?" asked Jack.

The twins nodded silently, feeling very guilty now. What a lot of work they had created from a little joke! They helped Mr Noodlenutt get all his heavy diving gear on and Jack and Dr Proctor carefully placed all the explosive equipment into a secure box.

The hatch was opened below into the outlet chamber, and the old diver disappeared. The hatch was immediately closed.

"We can watch him on the camera link," explained Dr Proctor.

They all sat down, Jack gave everyone coffee from his huge flask and the doctor produced delicious ginger cookies covered in toasted seeds from Mrs Magill's. She had brought them round that very morning.

"You might like these today." She had smiled, handing him the wrapped package. "Toasted valerian seeds are very good for nerves, I'm told." And she had disappeared back to her bakery.

The shadowy figure encased in the diving helmet, suit and boots moved across the screen. After a while the buzzer sounded, making everyone jump.

"It's okay, it's the outer door opening, Noodlenutt's coming back. He's got to re-pressurise."

Sure enough, eventually the hatch opened and they helped him take his helmet off and then the boots. He climbed into the cabin looking worried.

"Everything okay?"

"No, not exactly," said Mr Noodlenutt, sitting on the edge of the seat. "I can't seem to remember the exact sequence of the wiring, and of course I must be 100% certain." He looked up at them all.

Dr Proctor poured him a mug of coffee and handed him two ginger cookies. "Have a few moments' rest. It's always a very tricky business wiring up explosives. You'll be alright, you're a bit rusty, that's all."

"You see, we are not very far from Col Boodle-Smith's jetty where *Duty* is moored up, don't want any accidents, do we?" Mr Noodlenutt munched thoughtfully on his biscuits. "Any more? These are scrumptious."

Not much was said. Nobody wanted to distract the old diver from his thinking. Jebs and Jago felt terrible. It all seemed a bit dangerous for an old tree trunk.

"Go through it again carefully," said Jack eventually, "tell me what you do first."

"Wire the cortex round the trunk, add a detonator to the end and wire the end to the trunk," replied Mr Noodlenutt.

"That seems right," Dr Proctor said, and Jack agreed.

"Yes, yes, I'm absolutely sure now." And Mr Noodlenutt took the last bite of his fifth biscuit and got up.

"Right, here goes, boots and helmet."

Many willing hands helped him on with the heavy gear. He disappeared again and was soon seen on the screen. A gargling voice was heard through the intercom.

"Wire the trunk… tape the detonators… wire up the timer… set the clock and my watch to exactly the same time. Done. Ready to leave bottom."

It had been a calm and precise operation. All the spectators were very relieved when he returned.

"Well done, sir!" Dr Proctor patted him on the back. "I knew you could do it. Until Fiesta then. Plenty of bangs during the firework display, eh?" and they all laughed.

"Put some lemonade in then," growled Crocco. "I'm dying of thirst here."

Jebs and Jago marvelled as Jack poured

the foaming green liquid into the tank with the black cap marked FUEL.

"Want to drive?" asked Mr Noodlenutt, and Jebs and Jago both nodded furiously.

They shared the return journey to Goodly Harbour, and as they surfaced it was clear that there were queues of people across at Little Rushing waiting for the two pleasure boats. The brothers groaned.

"You've only got yourself to blame," laughed Jack. "Come on, only two days left, then peace and quiet as your serpent slips away!"

Each returned to their own duties around the town. Dr Proctor had several full trainloads to cope with and Jack had to keep Captain Lively up to date.

Mr Noodlenutt and Crocco gently drove up the slipway to the boathouse. After a hot bath and a change of clothes, the old gentleman sat outside his cottage with his favourite pipe. Mrs Magill could see him from the bakery window. He always sat on that seat with his pipe when he was thinking. All of a sudden

Jack appeared.

"Sorry to bother you, sir, just a small problem has arisen."

When Jack arrived back at the harbour office, Lucas Lively was in his office with an irate Minister for the Environment on the phone.

"My scientists want to take over the search for this creature. They are all very excited about it. A group of them are coming tomorrow by train to continue the investigations and you will no longer be in charge of this operation. You are to put your boats and your staff at their disposal. Do you understand, Lively? This could be a historic discovery."

"Yes, sir." Captain Lively stood up. "Will it be—"

The line went dead with a click just as Jack entered the office.

"Blast!" Lucas hit the desk top with his fist.

"Trouble, sir?"

"Bloomin' bureaucrats telling me what to do!" and he explained everything to Jack.

"Hmmmm." This certainly was a bit of a problem.

"Leave them to me, sir. You've got enough to do with the Fiesta and all the VIP guests."

"Yes, I have," agreed Lucas wearily.

Jack's mind was racing; he needed to see Mr Noodlenutt and Dr Proctor urgently and time was very short. He hurried along the lakeside to Eight Bells Cottage where he found who he was looking for. After he had explained the situation, both men sat staring across the large expanse of lake: the empty lake with nothing in it, and nothing to find… but, it didn't have to be empty, did it?

Mr Noodlenutt sat up straight and stopped puffing on his pipe.

"If those scientists are coming here to look for something then we'd better give them something to find, hadn't we Jack? Something more impressive than an old log, eh?"

Jack nodded, smiling.

"Yes, yes, you're quite right."

"And I know the very person to discover such a sea serpent," laughed Mr Noodlenutt.

"Yes you do, sir, and he's not very far from here, either," smiled Jack.

He jumped up.

"I'll leave this in your capable hands, sir. If I don't know much about this, then I don't have to tell any lies."

And shaking the old man's hand, he sauntered off up the quayside, whistling. Both he and Mr Noodlenutt knew Dr Proctor was a genius at making things out of the most unlikely rubbish.

# Chapter 9

# The Croccogooseygatersaurus

Later that evening over at Little Rushing on the Water, the two men got together in the railway shed where Dr Proctor lived with Peppi and Franki. Inside the workshop were boxes stacked with amazing treasures and finds that other people threw away, and the doctor had been collecting for years. Laid out were some interesting items: an old alligator-skin handbag, a long wooden African club with a round hard end, a pair of stuffed geese, rather tufty and bald-looking, a battered crocodile-skin suitcase, and a small pair of wooden paddles. Mr Noodlenutt laughed and laughed.

"I see where you're coming from, my friend! Not bad, not bad. I've brought my books, *Myths and Fabled Beasts*, *The Age of the Dinosaur*, and *Mammals of the Field and River*. I think we can make a start, don't you?"

Together they stripped the skin off the old suitcase and took the handbag to pieces. Somebody long ago had thought it very smart to have the small head and small feet folding over to make the clasp. It was a hideous example of bad taste, but a very lucky find.

As dawn broke, both men yawned and sat down heavily. Dr Proctor put the kettle on and made them a thick hot chocolate each. Yawning, they went outside with their steaming cups to watch the sunrise over the lake.

On the work bench lay the strangest but most realistic creature. Can you imagine what it looked like? Have you put all the pieces together to make a sea serpent? I wonder if you have. It was a *Croccogooseygatersaurus*; a glued, stitched, very scary prehistoric monster that had been created overnight: a small alligator's head with a goose skull, neck and body bones with the feathers still on; the four feet of the alligator, crocodile skin covering the hard African club making it into a long tail, and the black paddle became a tail fin. Only the goose feet had not been used. It was carefully stuck together with disgusting thick glue made from boiled bones. Every joint was covered in the thin crocodile skin from the suitcase and it looked a wonder to behold.

The idea was to carry him carefully inside Crocco under the lake and then release him before the scientists started their search in *Lionheart*. Jack would be navigating the harbour launch and he would find the Croccogooseygatersaurus quite quickly, in case he started to fall apart. That, hopefully, would be the end of that. Everyone would be happy and they would all go away, leaving them to enjoy the fiesta and blow up the log which had caused such a sensation. Easy, or so you would think.

Mr Noodlenutt and Dr Proctor sipped their hot chocolate, watching streaks of pink invade the watery blue sky. They were exhausted.

"Let's put little Crocco into big Crocco and we can go to bed," joked Mr Noodlenutt.

Inside, the remains were cleared up, the floor was swept, and their invention was wrapped in a large sheet and carried carefully into the snoozing car and tucked safely inside.

Both men yawned their goodbyes, and clapped each other on the back in congratulations, each longing for his bed.

Driving up the slipway at Eight Bells Cottage, the delicious smell of freshly baked bread was in the air. "I'm so hungry," thought Mr Noodlenutt, but before he could even step out of his car Mrs Magill knocked on the bubble roof.

"Can I come in?" She asked so charmingly and with such a sweet smile that without a thought he opened the passenger door. She stepped in at once, package in hand,

and sat down next to the long sheet-wrapped thing, which she totally ignored.

"Just a breakfast sandwich to keep you going, you've had such a long night. Been over at Dr Proctor's?" She opened the paper.

"Yes, and I'm so very hungry and weary."

He sighed. He was too tired to move.

"Eat up, then." She patted his knee. "Then you must sleep."

She got up to go, but shook her floury apron out and a cloud of white flour dust blew all around the cabin, and some landed on the sheet. Mr Noodlenutt ate his bacon, egg and mushroom hot baguette and promptly fell asleep in the comfortable seat of his car. Mrs Magill put her hand in her pocket and sprinkled just a little more flour over the sheet. Then she tiptoed out of the car and back into the bakery. She smiled to herself as she looked out of the window at the sleeping man inside the car.

"He's getting too old for such antics," she thought.

The next morning, Crocco and Mr Noodlenutt were positioned up at the far end of the lake by the hydro-electric station, waiting for a signal from Dr Proctor that the scientists had arrived. The group would travel in *Trooper* across the lake to Goodly Harbour, where Captain Lively would meet them and hand them over to Jack to be escorted to *Lionheart*, the launch. Peppi and Franki always pulled the steam whistle as the train left the station but instead of two toots there would be four, just to be sure that Mr Noodlenutt could hear it. Then the Croccogooseygatersaurus would be released from the hatch and float into the dark waters of the lake, hopefully to the surface – it was important the creature did not get snagged or stuck anywhere.

When he was sure all was in place, Crocco would motor back home and Mr Noodlenutt would have to wait patiently for the scientists to discover the elusive serpent of the lake. There had been so much talk and speculation about it that hopefully this would be the end of it. Just the fuses to detonate on

the night of the Fiesta fireworks, and with a
bang all would be sorted.

In the small galley kitchen was a
cardboard box tied with whiskery string.
Inside, Mr Noodlenutt found two large
ginger-seeded cookies. "Oh good, two left."
He munched them slowly, watching through
the window as the underwater life of the lake
swam past him. Then he heard the echo-like
toot of a whistle far away; he counted 2-3-4,
then – nothing.

"Got to be *Trooper*, we're on the way!" he
thought excitedly. He was just a little nervous.
"It will all be fine, nothing can go wrong," he
calmed himself, as the seeds from the cookies
released their soothing relaxing charms.

He looked at his special underwater
wristwatch with its bright-green hands. He set
the alarm for one hour and lay back in his seat
to wait. The timing was everything.

Back at Goodly Harbour there was great
excitement as the scientists hurried to get
aboard *Lionheart*, loading underwater
listening equipment, and underwater cameras.

There were sound recording and film experts, zoologists and marine biologists. Poor Jack was overwhelmed by his important passengers. Luckily the weather was reasonable – cloudy with a light breeze and no rain forecast. The catering company delivered a large picnic, and just as the launch was ready to go, Mrs Magill arrived with an enormous spicy seedcake decorated with chocolate shells, toasted seeds and glittering starfish. She handed the box to Jack.

"My contribution," she smiled. "Keep it just for the guests, our Goodly Harbour hospitality."

"Certainly, Mrs Magill, how kind of you," he thanked her.

Captain Lively watched them go from his harbour office window. He felt a great weight roll off his shoulders. Thank goodness for Jack, he would do it and do it well. He buzzed Jenny.

"Coffee and a croissant would be nice?" he requested, as she answered straight away.

"Is that croissants all round, sir?"

"Oh, why not!" he replied, "send Fred

along to Mrs Magill's."

"Will do," came the delighted voice of the office manager. "He must have come into some money!" she thought.

As he travelled up the lake, Jack kept an extra keen eye out. What were they going to see? It was quite exciting.

When Mr Noodlenutt heard the alarm go off on his watch, he jumped up at once and dressed in his diving gear. Unwrapping the long creature, he opened the hatch into the sealed compartment and pulled it carefully behind him. Then opening the door to the lake's dark waters, he and his companion floated outside. Crocco held the course and waited patiently. Letting go of the creature that he and Dr Proctor had created, Mr Noodlenutt watched it rising upwards like a ghost through the water to the light above. No obstacles barred its way. As it gathered speed upwards and disappeared from his view, the strangest thing happened. From below, it looked as if the creature flicked its tail from side to side, almost as if it was swimming.

Then… it was gone!

Feeling just a little sad, Mr Noodlenutt returned to the welcoming lights of his beloved vehicle waiting on the bottom of the lake. Opening the sealed hatch door and removing his helmet, suit, and boots, he sat in the warm cabin thinking about what he had seen.

"Everything going to plan?" asked Crocco.

"Just perfect. Only a matter of time, and Jack will pick him up."

"Good job done then. Any lemonade?"

Sitting on his boat, moored up on the lakeside, Col Boodle-Smith was having his morning sloe gin and biscuit. "This is the life." He chuckled to himself. It was almost time for his daily signal to Sgt Huff in the police station. As he surveyed the lake, a dark object came into view. A head and a long neck appeared in the distance, then it circled and went in the opposite direction. Small wavelets gently rocked *Duty* and lapped at the edges of the jetty.

"Crikey! What was that?"

He edged closed to the window and finally finding his binoculars he went out on deck for a better look. He could only see a small shape getting further and further away. "It could be that serpent!" he told himself, so excited at what he had seen that he rocked the boat as he blundered about.

"It might try to attack me." And he searched for his old army pistol. Now, we all know that the old colonel shouldn't have had a gun, let alone an old one, and what was even worse was that he had, hidden away, some ammunition that he had never told anyone about. Rummaging about in the locker, he found the clip of bullets. They were very old indeed, but Col Boodle-Smith quickly loaded the gun. He went outside; there was no sign of the serpent.

The Croccogooseygatersaurus was enjoying himself. He stretched his little legs and flicked his tail; he turned somersaults and popped out of the water with a splash. The special ingredients in Mrs Magill's flour had certainly worked on him! He was the only one of his kind, and certainly the only one there would ever be; he was making the most of his short life.

Jack had reached Col Boodle-Smith's jetty and passed by with his passengers all hanging over the side with their equipment buzzing and clicking. The colonel shouted out across the water,

Hey Jack, I've just seen it! It was going that way!" and he pointed up to the top of the lake. "Watch out, it could be dangerous!"

Jack waved in acknowledgement, not really understanding but very curious. He wondered what would happen next.

Under the lake Mr Noodlenutt was also wondering what was happening. Would Jack find the creature? Could the scientists be fooled by their invention? Had it fallen apart, or worse, filled with water and sunk down into the depths of the lake? He had to find out. "Let's go, Crocco, no point waiting about here. Surface and go very slowly back to the town."

Crocco obeyed at once and Mr Noodlenutt took up his position in the driving seat, the underwater camera switched on in front of him.

On the jetty, Col Boodle-Smith sent his daily message to Sgt Huff in Morse code. It was 10.30am exactly. He flashed away in great excitement.

*SIGHTING OF SERPENT AT 10.05. AM OBSERVING CLOSELY. HARBOUR LAUNCH IN PURSUIT.*

At the police station Sgt Huff received the message. "That crazy old coot," he thought, "he's seeing things. I have my own ideas about that so-called sea serpent. A good advertising trick, I'd say. Probably Jebs and Jago." He sniffed. "I'm not even going to reply to it. There's all this extra traffic to attend to these days, the town is swamped."

Slowly, as Crocco began to surface, a creature passed by on the screen. It had four little clawed feet and a long tail that flicked backwards and forwards. Then the strange goose body and at last the head, which looked straight at the screen full on… its eyes alive and moving! Mr Noodlenutt was startled and nearly jumped out of his seat. He strained his eyes nearer to the screen for a closer look but the face disappeared as the head turned round and the tail flashed by and vanished from view.

"It can't be." Mr Noodlenutt was absolutely stunned. "It just can't be. How could it have come alive? It looked so real. Did you see it, Crocco?"

"Yes, I did. It was definitely swimming, and it can do somersaults too," said Crocco's deep voice. "That's quite something."

"Dr Proctor must see this, we have to go and get him," decided Mr Noodlenutt at once. "Let's go. We'll stay under the water I think, out of Jack's way."

There was no explanation possible. The poor man was thoroughly shaken.

"It just can't be true," he kept telling himself, "it can't be," over and over again until he reached Goodly Harbour.

Out in the lake, the Croccogooseygatersaurus was getting better and better at swimming, diving and somersaulting. He was really enjoying himself. If he went quite deeply down into the water, then turned around and headed to the surface in a straight line, he could jump right out of the water with a swoosh! It was great fun. Unfortunately, it was only a matter of time before somebody spotted him. That somebody was Jack. He couldn't believe his eyes. "Is that what I'm looking for? But what *is* it?" He was extremely puzzled. "What am I supposed to do?"

Then everybody else saw it too. Gasps and shrieks and pandemonium followed, as equipment and people tripped over each other to get to the boat's edge. The harbour launch tipped dangerously as so many people leaned over on one side.

"Steady now," called Jack, "you must stay calm and sit down. I shall circle so that we can all see. Sit down! Now!" he told them, with great authority.

Most people obeyed him. Just one or two annoying scientists didn't. Then little Crocco (for that is what we shall call him now), swam across the wake of the boat, the water fizzing as it burst out of the engine. This was even better fun and he zig-zagged behind the launch from side to side. The passengers screamed with excitement.

"Isn't this incredible?" they shouted to each other.

Jack slowed down, scratching his head.

"What can I do now? Catch it? I don't know where Mr Noodlenutt and Dr Proctor got this from but it's certainly what all those boffins wanted to see."

With that, little Crocco dived under the water, frightened by the flash photography. He swam away and disappeared again from sight.

When Mr Noodlenutt arrived at the harbour he ran out of his vehicle to wait for the next train to arrive. He watched anxiously until he heard the steam whistle blow. "Oh good, he's on the way! Thank goodness."

And after five minutes, *Trooper* clanged noisily into the station. Mr Noodlenutt leapt into the driver's cab.

"You've got to come with me, Doc, you simply must! Our creature has come alive!"

"What? You're mad! Are you ill, Noodlenutt?" Dr Proctor put his hand on his friend's forehead.

"No, no, I don't think so. Please just come with me *now*!" he begged.

"Alright, alright."

First, Dr Proctor chalked on the blackboard the time of the next train. He allowed two hours. Then both men hurried back to the patient crocodile car. After they were seated, Crocco raced off back up the lake.

"Now what's all this about, my dear friend? You seem in a bit of a state."

"I think we'll make our way under the lake – it might be better – then I'll tell you."

Crocco dived below the water as instructed, where everything became tranquil and dreamy and silent. The explanation went like this:

"I followed our plan to the letter. I took the creature out and accompanied it to the surface, checking for obstacles, and I watched it float away. Everything was fine. When I got back into the car I saw something on the screen; something swam past me with four little legs and a long tail, then it turned around and looked right at me. Its eyes were alive, and so was the rest of it. Then it disappeared. I know it's complete madness!"

"Well, well, I really don't know what to say. Of course I believe you, but I would like to see it for myself, you understand I'm sure."

He smiled and patted his friend on the back reassuringly. "Then you shall."

Mr Noodlenutt began move Crocco upwards. What awaited him on the surface did not please him. Jack was circling in the harbour launch with a great crowd of people, who were noisily trying to get pictures and film of the creature.

Col Boodle-Smith had taken to the water in *Duty* and was racing up and down at great speed, shouting and waving every time little Crocco broke the surface. Dr Proctor sat motionless as he strained his eyes to see first the head, then the body, and the tail followed. It flipped over, somersaulting with a splash, and dived below the water. It was real, this creature he and Mr Noodlenutt had created on is workbench. The impossible had become reality. There could be no explanation; it was unfathomable. Dr Proctor was mesmerised as little Crocco came nearer to them and swam alongside quietly. Both inventors had a great view of him.

At that moment Col Boodle-Smith came roaring towards them, shouting, "Don't be afraid! I'm going to get him!" and the old soldier took aim and fired his gun at little Crocco. Bullets flew across the water, landing near the harbour launch. Some people screamed.

Jack was furious. "Stop firing, colonel! Stop firing!"

"We mustn't let him shoot it," whispered Mr Noodlenutt, "not now." And the chase began.

It was chaos – Col Boodle-Smith was like a man possessed. The boats sped about trying to avoid each other as Jack tried desperately to stop *Duty* and look after his own passengers. He was worried one of them might get shot so he radioed to Sgt Huff to scramble the lifeboat before either a death or a collision. Mr Noodlenutt and Dr Proctor tried to come between little Crocco and *Duty* but when the creature submerged they didn't know where he would pop up again.

Col Boodle-Smith knew he was running out of ammunition so was keen to make the last two bullets count. He would be a hero again, just like in the war. Slowing down, he took a wild guess where little Crocco would re-appear. Taking aim, he rested the pistol on his outstretched arm and waited. As the head broke the surface he fired twice and the gun clicked – it was empty.

There was a sort of strangled cry, then a hushed silence. Little Crocco stopped swimming and lay still; his tail flicked from side to side, then it too was motionless. The creature filled with water, and before anyone could reach it, sank slowly down into the water.

"You stupid old fool!" yelled a furious Jack, "You're under arrest!"

"What? Me? I've saved you all from that

154

dastardly serpent terrorising our lake! I shot it! You should be thanking me, and don't call me stupid!" the old colonel shouted back angrily.

Poor Dr Proctor and Mr Noodlenutt were in anguish; their miracle was over. Crocco dived below the water to search for the body of the dear little Croccogooseygatersaurus. It was a terrible disaster. He wasn't hard to find and the old diver dressed again in his diving gear and stepped outside sadly, to gather up the body in his arms. He brought the dripping creature inside the vehicle and laid him on the sheet, first drying him gently and then closing his eyes. Eventually the two inventors were brave enough to have a good long look at him.

"We made an amazing creature, didn't we?" said Dr Proctor quietly.

"He enjoyed his short life," nodded Mr Noodlenutt, a tear slipping down his face.

"Once we have blown up the log, I'll try to forget about the whole thing."

"Yes, my friend, I agree."

Dr Proctor wrapped up little Crocco and drove the submersible car back to Goodly

Harbour, both men deciding to stay on the surface all the way down the lake as a final farewell tribute to their incredible creation.

By now Sgt Huff had arrived in the lifeboat and he and Jack surrounded *Duty* on both sides. Col Boodle-Smith was duly arrested for illegal possession of a firearm and ammunition, discharging his pistol and endangering life, plus threatening behaviour. The old man was taken back to the police station in handcuffs.

Jack escorted the police launch, towing *Duty* behind him. The passengers were very shocked and frightened by what had happened right in front of their eyes.

"Let's have some tea," Jack offered them all. "Also, we've got that lovely spicy seedcake Mrs Magill gave us. Get the kettle on, Jim, and cut that cake up."

So Jim the harbour assistant did just that. It took everyone's mind off the mindless slaughter they had witnessed. In fact, by the time the launch reached Goodly Harbour, most of them strangely seemed to have forgotten about it and were all sitting quietly.

"There's none left for us," moaned Jim, as a Japanese lady greedily took the last piece, the crumbs and the spilt seeds which were California poppy seeds, known for their special properties.

"Never mind, Mrs Magill did say it was only for the guests, Jim. She's left us some iced buns back at the office. She really is a treasure."

"Don't like the look of this weird bunch of boffins, Jack. What's up with them?"

Curiously, the scientists were all swaying together, eyes closed, rocking to the rhythm of the boat.

"Probably delayed shock," said Jack. "They were all a bit hysterical."

# Chapter 10

# A not-so-sad ending

At the police station, all the evidence was being gathered. The gun and empty bullet clip were in a plastic bag and poor old Col Boodle-Smith was in deep trouble.

Sgt Huff felt furious he had missed all the excitement.

"I did send you a message," accused the colonel, "but you didn't reply. You could have helped me, and maybe I wouldn't have killed it. Maybe I shouldn't have killed it. Help me out, Otto, won't you, there's a good fellow? I don't want to go to prison." He became very sad and sorry for himself.

"Should have thought of that sooner," was the cold policeman's reply.

The scientists were all taxied to the Harbour View Hotel in the town to await interview and did not return to the train, but Dr Proctor had to make two journeys to convey all the many bystanders back to Little Rushing. He was inconsolable. He had never felt so sad in his life; a triumph and a disaster all in one day.

The next morning when Sgt Huff turned up at the hotel to interview all the witnesses, not one of them could remember exactly what had happened. It was very strange.

"Don't you want to find the body of the serpent and take it back to the Natural History Museum?" the director was asked.

"No, no I don't think so." He smiled vaguely, with staring eyes. "Just let it all rest in peace now. Best thing." And he smiled the weird smile again.

Sgt Huff could not quite understand it.

As a result, the body of the serpent stayed with Mr Noodlenutt, who had laid it carefully on the boathouse floor beside Crocco, covered in a white sheet. He and Dr Proctor had dinner together that evening at Eight Bells Cottage, and then they sat outside with their freshly brewed coffee. In a while Mr Noodlenutt lit his pipe. The evening was warm, soon the light was fading; everything was still and the town clock struck 10.00 p.m.

What a lot of comings and goings the clock had seen this week all over the town! Just then he saw Mrs Magill come out of the bakery and quietly walk along the quayside. She tiptoed into the boathouse and shook her apron over the white sheet. A little cloud of flour gently sank to the floor. Smiling with satisfaction, she strolled outside.

"Good evening, gentlemen," she said quietly, "may I join you?"

"Mrs Magill! How very nice to see you." Both men stood up at once. "Come and join us."

161

She accepted their invitation and sat down on the long wooden seat. "Quite a day!" she remarked softly.

"Indeed." Dr Proctor gazed into the distance.

"Unimaginable." Mr Noodlenutt puffed pungent billows of smoke from his pipe.

"I expect it has all been for the best," Mrs Magill ventured. "Things are never what they seem."

"Coffee, Mrs Magill?" inquired Dr Proctor.

"That would be lovely, thank you."

And soon he had fetched a steaming cup for her and sat down again. Then there was a slight rustle behind them, and as they turned around, a familiar shape trailing a crumpled white sheet slid down the slipway and plopped into the smooth shiny water; little ripples broke the surface. Mr Noodlenutt clutched Dr Proctor's arm.

"What was that? It wasn't... it couldn't be...?" But even as he whispered the words, a small black head popped up, then a long neck; two eyes stared at them, blinked several times, and croaking a strangled, gurgling noise, it vanished beneath the water. A tail that looked just like a black paddle broke the surface, flipped over with a splash, and was gone. It had taken about 50 seconds from start to finish.

Mrs Magill beamed. "There you are, just as I said. Nothing is what it seems." She drained her coffee cup, stood up and said, "I must be off to bed, gentlemen. Goodnight, and sleep well. You've had a busy day."

And she left the two open-mouthed, to contemplate what had happened. They were still sitting there when she turned her bedroom light off.

"Men!" She shook her head with a smile of satisfaction.

That is almost the end of the story of the Serpent of the Lake, but I know you will want to know what happened to silly old Col Boodle-Smith. He was locked up in the police station for several days and fined a good deal of money for having an illegal firearm. For his threatening behaviour and destroying an endangered species, he had to do Community Service for six months. This consisted of helping with the dustbins every Tuesday and serving lunch at the Old People's Home on Fridays. He really was very lucky he did not go to prison, after none of the scientists could remember much about that day.

Luckily for him, neither Jack nor Sgt Huff had the heart to give evidence against him. In the end Sgt Huff realised he should have answered the Morse code message and he also should have confiscated the gun the last time that old soldier was in trouble. Mr Noodlenutt informed the harbour authority and the police that he had found the remains of the creature and there had been a burial at sea early one morning.

On the night of the Fiesta fireworks Crocco, Mr Noodlenutt and Dr Proctor travelled up the lake quietly, and during the finale of splendid rainbow-coloured rockets which lit up the skies with glittering sparkles and noisy bangs, there was one very loud bang at the end. Bits of wooden debris showered the lake and sadly a large hole was blown in *Duty*,

Col Boodle-Smith's boat. She filled slowly with water and sank miserably to the bottom. Mr Noodlenutt and Dr Proctor smiled at each other. They had got their revenge.

Gradually the town returned to normal, and the serpent of the lake was forgotten by everyone, except the two great friends who had created it. One day perhaps its humped back might be seen on the lake's dark waters again, who can say?

# ADVENTURE FOUR

## Chapter 11

# The Castle of Charlemagne

I f you are patient and read on, the story will become clear to you. You will probably wonder what this has to do with Mr Noodlenutt and Crocco. It is quite exciting, as all their adventures are.

Long, long ago, the Duke of Charlemagne ran away from his own country and built a small castle on the edge of the lake, not far from Little Rushing. He had displeased the Pope and had to go into hiding in case he had his head cut off. The sheltered inlet the duke had discovered was the ideal site for his castle, between two cliffs, because it was not a very easy place to get to and therefore a perfect place to hide.

Local carpenters and builders thought he was a bit mad to choose such a difficult location, but he paid very well and eventually the castle was finished. It was small and neat and could only be seen from the water, wedged perfectly between the cliffs. The lake lapped at the wooden jetty where boats could tie up, and a bridge led to the castle entrance. A steep flight of steps led up behind the castle walls to the top of the hill, where a barn was built for stables and a store.

The duke lived there for many years with only a few faithful servants, and because he was lonely, he took up woodcarving to pass the time, carving intricate patterns, small animals into the beams, flowers and leaves around the big wooden beds, and lions and dragons on the staircase. He became an excellent carver and because he was always frightened that somebody would find him he built a secret room under the stairs which was perfectly hidden in the carvings. If you turned the lion's head, the door opened; press the dragon's foot and the floor slid back to reveal a narrow staircase. The staircase led to a room with a hidden spyhole window to look out over the lake. An iron handle pulled a square of stone out to check for intruders below the castle.

This secret room had a bed built into the wall, with cosy curtains that pulled all around it. It was furnished with a table and chair, and a fireplace with a cooking pot hung from hooks above it. A trap door in the floor led to the lake and water could be hauled up by bucket from an opening beside the stone sink. Little sacks of dried food were stored on shelves around the walls; books, pen and parchment lay on a small desk. Candles, holders and a tinderbox stood neatly on the wooden dresser, with plates and dishes. The duke had thought of everything during his long time in exile.

He even carved two smiling faces over the fireplace so he wouldn't feel alone. Nobody ever came looking for the duke, and eventually he died a very old man, and of course all his secrets died with him. The servants left, and the castle stood empty and dark for a long, long time.

\*\*\*

Mr and Mrs Glum who ran the ticket office at Little Rushing station had some bad news one morning. Mr Glum's brother, Reginald, had to go away with his wife for a week and needed somebody to look after their children. Reginald knew if he asked his brother he would say no, so he put Theodore and Arabella on the bus with a large picnic and two labels around their necks:

*To be delivered to Little Rushing by the Water ticket station.*

He gave the driver a canvas bag and put £20 in Theodore's pocket.

"Off you go, don't get off the bus for any reason. Mum and I will see you next week.

'Bye kids, you're going to have a great time…"

"…not," he told himself, feeling very sorry for his two lovely children setting off into the lions' den, which is what he and his wife Annie May called the Glums' house. Then he rang his brother.

Now, Theodore and Arabella were twins. They were very good children, rather clever and very fond of history and stories about long ago, kings and queens, castles and knights and dragons, so of course they had got several books from the library about the history of the lake and its two villages. Arabella made a list of the places she wanted to visit and Theodore found out the names of important people, saints, churches and castles in the area on the bus journey.

As the bus motored along, they munched on the enormous picnic their mother had packed into a wicker basket: egg sandwiches, ham sandwiches, sausage rolls, squares of cheese, marmite swizzles, apples, pears, bananas and large portions of sticky toffee pecan cake, washed down with two bottles of green lemonade. Just as they had finished making their lists and eating all the food, the bus drew up outside Little Rushing station.

"We're here! That didn't take long," said Theodore cheerfully.

"No, only two and a half hours," added Arabella, shaking the crumbs from her blue spotted napkin and folding everything into the wicker basket.

The driver, whose name was Arthur, climbed out carrying the large canvas bag. Theodore packed his leather satchel with the books and notebooks and looked around with interest.

"Righty ho," said Arthur cheerily, "this is you, my dears."

He glanced around quickly in case the Glums came out. He'd met the Glums before and he wasn't keen to see them again.

"Must he going, look after yourselves. Don't get eaten by any dragons, will you? I hear there are some strange animals in these parts."

And he shook them both by the hand and hopped back into his bus. He was gone in a roar of exhaust fumes in less than 60 seconds.

"Well, here we are," said Theodore. "Is that the lions' den?" and he pointed to the house next door to the sus station.

"Shuuuuush!" Arabella put her finger to her mouth. "You mustn't say that, it's only Dad's joke, you know."

She adjusted her red knitted beret and picked up the basket.

"Here goes, bravely onward into battle."

And she marched ahead, leaving her brother to struggle with the heavy canvas bag and his satchel.

"Wait, I'm coming," he called.

She made for the station door and peeped in. Two very miserable people stared back at her, with mousey hair, glasses and a strong stare.

"Yes?"

"We're Arabella and Theo."

"Oh yes?"

"You know, Reginald's children?

Theo spoke a bit louder. "We are expected… definitely."

"Come here."

Mr Glum peered through the misty glass

173

and squinted at the labels tied neatly round their necks as the children approached nervously

"I suppose you must be. This is not convenient, you know, not convenient at all. We're not used to children," spoke Mrs Glum.

"Do you eat a lot?" asked Mr Glum sharply.

"Um, well, not much, you know," stammered Arabella.

"That's good then, neither do we."

Mrs Glum pushed a key through the ticket office window.

"Here you are. Go inside, it's the cottage next door, 'Haven's Rest'. Your bedroom is in the attic. Call us when you have made the supper."

"That's after you have done the cleaning of course. You've got to earn your keep," added Mr Glum, as his wife slammed the widow shut and he pulled down the blind over the window.

The children left the ticket office and went round to the cottage door. Theodore put the key in the lock and opened the grey-painted door. A cold, dark, damp smelling house lay before them, rather uninvitingly. A large spider let itself down its thin web and ran away across the floor and out of the door.

"Even the spiders don't like it," said Arabella. "Come on, we'll soon liven this place up. I've got my radio with me."

They crept up the stairs, which was difficult because there were piles of magazines and newspapers on every tread. Cobwebs brushed their faces and the windows were thick with dust.

"Yuck."

"Double yuck."

The children held on to each other as they climbed the stairs, which were covered in a faded orange mottled sticky covering. Nobody could call this a carpet. At the top a creaky door led to a very disappointing guest room; plain walls, bare floorboards and two iron beds with thin sheets and hospital covers, which were surprisingly clean. A wardrobe and a chest of drawers were the only furniture. When Arabella rubbed the dirty window pane she could see behind the station and all the way up the lake for a long way.

"There's a great view! I'll clean the window." She got out her hanky, spat on it, and soon the view was better. Pushing the stiff window open together, lovely fresh air blew in.

"Let's do our chores and then we can go out and explore. Come on!" suggested Theo brightly, so putting their few belongings away they went down to see the kitchen and the rest of the house. It was simply awful. Worse than they had imagined: dusty, dark and miserable.

"Just like them!" laughed Arabella.

She turned the radio on full blast, tied her hair up in a bandana, and rolled up her sleeves. "We'll be out of here in half an hour, I promise."

And so they were. Brushed, dusted, wiped and polished, the small house lay gleaming. A salad of lettuce, tomatoes and ham was plated up. It was very simple because there wasn't anything else. Laughing to each other, they were ready to explore Little Rushing.

Arabella, who was never daunted, took the key back to the station.

"It's all ready, Auntie," she told an expressionless Mrs Glum. "We're off exploring now, 'bye." And she turned and fled before Mrs Glum could even open her mouth.

Mr Glum's eyes became smaller and he set his mouth in a stubborn snarl. "Hmmmmm." He made a sort of noise. "She's an uppity piece if ever I saw one. Let's go and see what is for our tea, my love."

# Chapter 12

# The children go sight seeing

Theo and Arabella ran for their lives up the hilly path out of the village, high above the railway station and along a sheep track which led into the forest. From here they had a wonderful view, not only of Little Rushing which lay below them, but also of Goodly Harbour spread out across the lake. Boats chugged up and down, the train whistle blew as it rattled across the bridge, and white clouds scudded by, as the clock chimed 5 o'clock. In the far distance a windmill turned and a tiny tractor moved across a brown field high on the hillside.

"Oh, I forgot to pick up my binoculars." Theo sucked his teeth angrily.

Arabella was entranced with the whole panorama spread out before her; it was like looking at a model village, everything was working perfectly.

"This is heaven," she told Theo. "We've got a lot to see, so let's walk for a while."

Setting off at a good pace, in an hour they had reached the hydro-electric station at the head of the lake, by the Whispering Falls. This was the locals' name for the huge waterfall which powered the turbines for the electricity. Wherever you were, you could hear the slight rushing of the water as it hurled itself over the steep precipice.

Sparky Watts and Bill Brightly were tidying up outside the large brick building. One was mending the fence and the other was painting the window frames, as proudly they kept the electric station neat and tidy at all times.

"Good evening." Both men greeted the boy and girl. "You've had a long walk," they said, knowing the two visitors could only have come down the steep rocky path through the forest. Not many people walked that far.

"Yes, it was rather exciting," Theo told them. "We've come from Little Rushing but we live in Bedcaster, which is a big town. This is wonderful," pointing to the waterfall.

"It is," agreed Sparky, "and it's useful too. It makes the electricity for the whole lake, we're very lucky."

Eventually the story came out, how they were the niece and nephew of Mr and Mrs Glum and staying for a week. Arabella told the two men of their passion for history and all the places they hoped to visit… Bonaventure Tower, St Ignatius Church, the ruined priory, King Alfred's Stones; she went on and on. Sparky and Bill listened politely. When she had finished, Bill scratched his head, thinking.

"Have you got the castle of the Duke of

Charlemagne on your list? I bet you haven't, hardly anyone knows about it," he told her proudly, winking at Sparky, who just smiled.

"No, no, I've never heard of it before," replied Arabella in surprise. "Where is it?"

"You've just walked past it!" laughed Sparky and Bill leaning on each other's shoulders, thinking this was a huge joke. The children looked very puzzled.

"It's hidden you see, that was the whole point of it," explained Bill. "When you get to the ruined barn on the top of the hill, look through the trees for a flight of stone steps. I expect the path is all grown over now but it's there, I promise you. Let us know if you find it."

And the two men went back to finish their work. They had a venison pie in the oven and didn't want it spoiled.

"Bye!" The children waved, "And thank you," Theo called.

In a flash they rushed back up the steep stony track, puffing at the top, and followed the path through the pine trees. It was cool and dry and smelled of lovely wood. Theo kept looking for the barn but the trees seemed to get in the way. They didn't find it and gave up, tired and hungry.

"We'll do it tomorrow, definitely," promised Arabella, more for herself that her brother. "We won't give up until we find it."

"No," agreed Theo, just a little less enthusiastic now he was starving. Eventually Haven's Rest came into view and they found one light on in the kitchen and the Glums finishing the salad – all the salad. They had eaten everything.

"We thought you weren't coming in for tea," sniffed Mrs Glum.

"It seemed a pity to waste it. Never mind, you can go and do the shopping tomorrow for us. Here is a chocolate biscuit for you both," said Mr Glum. He unlocked a tin with a picture of an old king and queen on it, and pulled out one ancient, crumbly biscuit. He looked at it. "I think it will be alright. Now off to bed with you, and don't keep the light on too long. Nighty night."

"I'll leave you a list and some money for the shopping. Go early if you want something for breakfast," snapped Mrs Glum.

"Yes, Auntie," replied Arabella.

She and Theo trudged wearily up the stairs.

"Old crow!"

"Skinny lizard!"

And they laughed to each other as they reached the bedroom where they shared the biscuit, and fetched a glass of water from the bathroom. Theo rummaged in his satchel and found two toffees, half a packet of crisps and an apple. Arabella found some crusts from her sandwiches and a piece of squashed cake, and together they ate the meagre supper. It was just about enough.

"We'll buy some supplies tomorrow with that money Dad gave us," Theo decided firmly. "I'm not starving for anybody, especially those old dragons. Wait 'till Dad knows."

In the morning, while the Glums snored away loudly behind their bedroom door, Theo and Arabella got up and crept downstairs. A five-pound note lay on the table with a very long list of shopping beside it.

"She's got to be bonkers!" snorted Theo. "That food will cost a lot more than this. Come on, let's go, I think the small passenger ferry has started already. At least we can have some breakfast!"

Arabella and Theo raced out of the door and down to the ferry pontoon. Crossing the lake early in the morning was an exciting journey for them, and as they reached the other side the smell of bacon and fresh toast was in the air.

"Mmm, that smells wonderful," both sniffing the delicious aroma. Following the smell, they found a café where people were sitting outside and others queued for breakfast. It was called 'Alf's'. Immediately, the twins joined the queue and it seemed to be a very jolly place indeed.

A young girl served them, saying, "Order, then find a table and we'll bring it to you. Name? Take your drinks with you."

Theo gave her the precious £20 note and picked up two glasses of freshly squeezed orange juice. It was a really friendly place with

French accordion music playing quietly in the background. Soon their plates arrived, and never had the two children enjoyed food so much. They couldn't even talk, just steadily munching away until their hunger had gone.

"More toast, Theo?" called the smiley girl from behind the counter.

"Yes, please!"

"Coming up!"

Four large slices arrived in a few minutes.

"Let's make sandwiches with these," suggested Arabella wisely, and four marmalade sandwiches were soon tucked away in their bag.

Reluctantly leaving the café, the search was on for a food store. A small market stall was open and the twins bought bread, cheese, butter, eggs and honey with their own money. It was too embarrassing to even offer the five pound note.

"It's too bad," sniffed Arabella. "They're so mean, we're not magicians. Let's explore."

They wandered up the lakeside cobbles, admiring the old cottages, boats and the quayside. Arriving outside Mrs Magill's cake shop, they gazed through the window at the glorious selection of chocolate cakes and gateaux, delicate light sponges, meringues, eclairs, and crunchy cookies and iced biscuits.

"Shall we?" asked Theo, wondering.

"Of course!" grinned Arabella. "We can't miss this!" and so both ventured into the warm shop that smelled deliciously of caramel.

"Let's buy a treat for Uncle and Auntie," said Arabella with a sudden rush of generosity. She really was a very kind girl at heart.

Mrs Magill stood smiling, smoothing her daffodil-flowered apron. In one corner of the shop was a green sparkling pyramid of lemonade bottles.

"Good, our favourite, two bottles of lemonade please, and four gingerbread biscuits, two men and two ladies!" laughed Theo.

"Very well, I'll box them for you in case they get broken," and a cardboard box and a stripy ribbon seemed to appear and tie itself up.

"Will that be all?" smiled Mrs Magill.

"Perhaps a small bag of flour? We could

make pancakes then, couldn't we Theo?" asked Arabella.

"Good idea."

Mrs Magill put everything in a firm bag and asked where they were from.

"Bedcaster, but we are staying at the railway station cottage over at Little Rushing, Haven's Rest," they told her. "Our parents are away for a week. We love it here. We're going to try and find the Duke of Charlemagne's castle today, do you know it?"

Mrs Magill smiled as usual. "I couldn't say I do. Just local stories one hears."

"Well, thank you, and we know where to get our lemonade now."

They waved goodbye and left the shop, the bell clanging on the door as they closed it.

"Poor dears," thought Mrs Magill, "life with those Glums must be hard. What lovely children to buy them a present, and how fortunate they found my shop!" And she smiled her very special smile to herself.

When Theo and Arabella arrived back at the cottage, they found the doors firmly locked, all the windows closed, and there was no way to get in. They ran round to the station but there was a strange man in the ticket office behind the counter.

"Where are Mr and Mrs Glum?" asked Theo politely.

"They have gone on the train to a meeting at the town hall, all about tourism and such like. There's a free lunch as well. I'm just helping out."

"Oh," replied Theo, very surprised.

"Let's go." Arabella tugged his arm, "We're leaving. Blow them both!" She was very angry. Passing the cottage, they left the £5 note sandwiched between two stones in the porch.

"We're taking this food, we paid for it, and we're not coming back. We'll find those two nice men we met yesterday. I expect we could stay with them." And she tossed her head. She was in quite a temper.

Theo wasn't sure about all this but really, what could they do? There was nowhere for them to go. Sharing the bags of food, they walked through the station, along the platform and out the other side.

Dr Proctor was polishing *Trooper* in the siding. He noticed the children walking by. "Good morning," he called. "Off for a walk?"

"Yes," replied Arabella coolly.

"Come and have a ride on my train when you've got a minute. *Trooper* and I would love to take you over to Goodly Harbour."

Pepperoni and Frankfurter greeted the children with a wag of their tails and a bark.

"We will," nodded the children, pleased that somebody liked them.

Off they went, following the signs to the Whispering Falls. Not many visitors took this path as it was very steep and rocky and not suitable for small children or pushchairs.

"We really must keep our eyes open today for the ruined barn and the steps," said Theo. "These bags are getting a bit heavy now."

Arabella ignored his complaints as she was keen to find them too.

"The castle can only have been built in an inlet," she reasoned, "it's the only possible place. So look for a cut in the cliffs, or a small valley. Or, we could split up, one walk along the top above the forest, looking for the barn, and one in the forest looking for the steps. What do you think?"

Theo wasn't sure.

"Let's just stay together, Bella. I'd rather we did that."

"Okay."

So they continued their walk, glimpsing the busy life on the lake through the trees. Eventually, tired by the climb, a rest became necessary and both sat down. Arabella looked all around her, scanning the cliffs below for a break in the contours. Theo watched some birds flitting among the branches; he thought they were long-tailed tits.

"Where have those birds gone?" he asked himself out loud. He stood up and took a few steps down the hilly, leafy slope, and came back smiling.

"Roll a stone down there, Bella." He pointed to the place.

She did as she was told and the stone rolled for a while, then it disappeared. Moments later a crash could be heard.

"There's an edge there, I'm sure of it.

Leave all the bags for a moment, we don't want to carry them. They'll be alright, nothing can happen to them."

He pulled her to her feet and very carefully they tiptoed and edged themselves farther down the hill. Something hard bumped Theo's foot. He leaned down and scrabbled in the leaves – an old stone step appeared.

"We've found them! What luck!"

They were both very excited. Getting a couple of stout sticks each, they set about uncovering all the debris, rotten leaves and mud from the old disused steps. It became obvious there was a building below them. Masses of young trees had grown since the duke had died and it was virtually grown over; just the roof could be seen.

"That's got to be it." Arabella pointed. "It's very overgrown."

"Do you think the Sleeping Beauty will be inside?" laughed Theo.

"Or a dragon?" suggested Arabella.

By whacking hard with their sticks they managed to hold back the brambles enough to be able to tread on the slippery, earthy steps. Eventually the rickety wooden entrance to the castle appeared out of the undergrowth of rhododendrons and hazel trees. It was eerily quiet. Theo noticed the birds he had seen perched together on the stone battlements, watching them. The great studded door was dark and menacing.

"That's not going to be open, is it? I expect the key was lost years ago." Arabella said sadly.

When they reached the huge door it was very firmly closed.

"Thought so, let's go round the other side."

Theo followed his sister round the top battlements to a stone flight of steps, which led downwards to another door with narrow windows either side. This door too was locked. One of the windows had no glass but bars across it; several were missing. Theo looked at Arabella, then grabbed a bar and pulled fiercely. Rusted beyond repair, it snapped at once. His sister did exactly the same, leaving a shower of rusty flakes all over the ground.

"That was easy!" laughed Theo, dusting off the metal flakes all over him. The window was now quite open, just enough room for a small person to climb in.

"Better get our stuff first."

So both quickly returned up the steps to collect their precious bags of food. Back at the dark, now open window they hesitated. What would they find inside?

"You first," Arabella said. "Go on!"

Theo bravely squeezed himself through the stone frame. He put his feet down gingerly onto a wooden floor. It was alright and seemed quite safe, just lots of dry leaves scattered about.

"Pass the bags, then you next."

Arabella soon followed. They both stood inside the castle, looking around. It was very dark but they made their way towards the distant light and began opening doors. Suddenly more daylight entered the castle at that moment, for the first time for 400 years. Each room was still furnished, if rather dusty.

"Not much worse that Auntie and

Uncle's and better furnished than Haven's Rest!" they laughed together.

The castle was exactly how the duke had left it: massive carved beds graced the bedrooms, with huge tapestries and grand curtains; stone fireplaces, and large beams with animals, birds, flowers and fishes carved onto every surface of the dark wood. It was fantastic. Far from scary, it felt a very friendly place. The children followed the large carved staircase down. There were only two floors and the battlements, so it was rather a small castle.

Descending into the living quarters, they discovered a large living room, an enclosed hall and a kitchen with attached scullery, with everything still in its place. Even the fireplace had ash in it, but above it, two faces smiled out at them, both wearing crowns. A pair of 'C's were entwined in the carving, with a little coronet above them. Arabella and Theo were absolutely entranced with the castle; it was just what they had never even hoped to dream of: their very own castle.

"Let's sit at the table and eat our lunch in style," suggested Arabella.

She opened her bag and took out some paper that the bread had been wrapped in and wiped down the dusty table and two of the chairs with red velvet seats. Theo fetched two silver plates off the dresser and wiped them on his sleeve.

"They're okay," he said. "Do you think there is any water in the kitchen?"

"We'll see, after we've eaten." Arabella was too hungry to worry about that.

They ate the bread and cheese and drank one bottle of the green lemonade between them from a pair of jewel-encrusted goblets.

"A meal fit for a king!" toasted Theo, raising his goblet. "Where is my crown? I seem to have lost it."

After lunch they went to explore the kitchen. There was an old iron pump for water set in the flagstone floor.

"Comes straight from the lake." Theo nodded. "How clever."

"Better boil it, then," frowned Arabella, thinking how dirty it could be.

The kitchen had a fireplace with iron hooks and an old rusty spit built over the fire.

Various cubby holes were fitted darkly into the chimney. One had an iron door hanging off its hinges.

"That'll be the bread oven." Arabella was pretty sure.

Blackened pots and pans lay on shelves. Stone-cut sinks stood in the scullery, carved out of large rocks. Everything worked and it would be possible to begin living again in this castle without any modern conveniences.

"Lights are the only thing we haven't got. They would have had oil lamps or candles."

"We could light the fire?" suggested Theo, eyeing Arabella to see what she thought.

"Yes, we could, but what if the chimney's blocked?"

"Let's look up inside and see if we can see some daylight."

The kitchen chimney had a bend in it so they couldn't tell about that one, but the living room fire went straight up into the daylight. Plenty of sticks and bird poo had fallen down into the fireplace but at least it wasn't blocked.

"We've got no matches," sighed Arabella.

"No, that's a problem."

They scratched their heads.

"Never mind, let's forget it." Theo looked at his watch. It was four o'clock.

"What a long time we've been."

"Do you think Auntie and Uncle will be back yet?"

"Probably." Theo frowned.

"I don't really care," said Arabella defiantly. "I think they are perfectly horrid, unkind and thoughtless. They haven't a clue about children. I hate them and I'm not going back. I'm going to be queen of this castle!" and she got up and flounced around.

Theo burst out laughing.

"Look at you, your Majesty. You'll soon go back when there's no food!" Theo was slightly worried inside. He knew Arabella could be very difficult when she made up her mind and her mind was very seriously made up now.

The sun came out and caught a chink of the thick glass, casting a jewelled beam on to the floor.

"I know how to light the fire!" and Theo

rummaged in his satchel for his small magnifying glass.

"Get those sticks arranged into a pyramid, Bella, don't worry about the bird poo – that burns well, it seems. Get me some paper, that old wrapping will do, and one of those silver plates. Quick, while the sun is still out!" He fired his orders at her.

So the paper and plate were placed beneath the sunbeam and the magnifying glass held between them. A small spot of light played on the paper; gradually as they watched, the spot turned brown, began to smoke, and hey presto! A flame appeared. Carefully, Theo carried the plate to the fireplace and when the rest of the paper was alight he set it gently into the sticks. They smoked and then crackled, and a hiss later, broke into flames!

"Well done!"

Bella admired his work. "We mustn't let it go out now."

"You're serious about staying here, aren't you?" ventured Theo.

"I certainly am," she replied at once.

"They probably won't even notice we've gone. Come on, let's go and get some more wood for this fire."

Outside they threw loads of sticks and bigger branches from the woods down onto the battlements and made a great pile. Then Theo jumped on all the small rotten ones and the two then carried armfuls down into the living room.

"Where's the toilet and the bathroom?"

"You must be joking!" answered Theo. "Water from the pump is what you wash in, and the privy, that's what it was called in the old days, that's off the scullery and goes straight into the lake."

"I'm not drinking that water, then!"

"We've got one bottle of lemonade left, but we can get the water from that stream if you want to. We could fill up the bottles."

Soon it was sorted in their minds, the basics of everyday living. The fire which hadn't been lit for years blazed and the smoke went up the chimney, and mercifully any bird's nests had rotted and fallen down into the fireplace. Of course, Arabella and Theo had forgotten that the smoke would come out of the top and spiral up into the air, and that people would notice it and wonder where it had come from.

# Chapter 13

# Leaving the Glums

S parky and Bill saw the wispy smoke curling over the top of the trees.

"Somebody's got a camp fire in the woods. Hope they're going to be careful. I'll keep my eye on it," Bill told himself.

Now, in actual fact the nearest house as the crow flies to the Castle of Charlemagne was Col Boodle-Smith's, down by the water.

He too only had access to his house by boat. As we know, he had been in disgrace, his boat sunk and his reputation rather tarnished. He was not spoken to by members of the harbour authority, and rather shunned by Mr Noodlenutt, Dr Proctor and Sgt Huff. All Morse code messages had ceased between him and the police station.

He was in his garden that afternoon trying to repair his boat. He noticed the smoke creeping through the trees, and it made him cough.

"Where the devil is that smoke coming from? Not campers again, wretched people." He coughed again, and the smoke got in his eyes.

By now, the Glums had returned from their free lunch, where they had drunk several free glasses of sherry, and had retired to bed with loud snoring. Poor old Derek had to man the ticket office all day. Of course, he never got paid, just kept getting promises of a large cheque and was given a free ticket for the train, but only on a wet Monday when nobody wanted to go anywhere. So the absence of their niece and nephew was not high on the list of priorities for Mr and Mrs Glum, which is rather shocking.

When it got dark, Theo and Arabella snuggled up by the fire, ate some bread, cheese and honey, which they toasted on long wooden sticks, and finished the lemonade. Arabella took one of the long curtains down and gave it a good shaking outside. Then she wrapped them both up in it and by the time the light from the fire faded, they were both asleep, thoroughly exhausted.

In the morning, the Glums woke up and didn't remember for at least half an hour about the children. Then it gradually dawned on them that they hadn't heard anyone moving about upstairs.

"Young people always stay in bed until lunchtime," Mrs Glum sniffed. "Leave them, dear."

So they did.

Later the phone rang. It was Reginald and Annie May to speak to their children.

"Oh, they're not up yet," Mr Glum told his brother. Do you want me to wake them?" When Reginald said no, Mr Glum agreed to another call at teatime, and they both rang off.

"Where's my shopping, I wonder?" asked Mrs Glum. "I expect they've spent my money on sweets. That's the sort of thing horrible children do."

But Mr Glum found the £5 note between the stones when he went to see the postman.

"Strange," he thought. "Is this your £5 note, dearest?" he called to his wife.

"What's the number?" and when he read it out to her, she replied, "That's definitely mine."

Mrs Glum then had a funny feeling come over her. Pains in her arms shot through her and she sank to the floor.

"Arnold! Arnold!" she called out, and promptly fainted.

By the time Mr Glum reached her she was out cold. He looked at his unconscious wife.

"I wonder what's wrong with her?"

Then he felt sharp shooting pains in his

own legs and he fell to the floor and fainted too. There was no sound from either of the Glums and they certainly didn't hear the phone ringing insistently in the hallway.

Back at the Castle of Charlemagne, Arabella and Theo were eating the gingerbread people for breakfast.

"To think I even bought them a treat each," remarked Bella. "I must have been having a funny five minutes. This is what I think of you, Auntie Edna." And she pulled each arm slowly off the gingerbread lady and ate them in several small bites.

"Now me!" laughed Theo, and he took the gingerbread man, broke both his legs off and crunched them up noisily.

They closed the box Mrs Magill had given them and looked for the empty bottles of lemonade to fill them up with clean water from the stream. When they found them, they stopped and stared: both the bottles were completely full again of sparkling, green lemonade!

"Where did they come from?"

"How very peculiar."

"How very convenient!" smiled Arabella in delight. "Shall we taste it?" Opening one slowly, Theo dipped his finger inside the bottle and licked it.

"Mmm. Just the same. Delicious!"

"Call it a miracle, then," and Arabella twirled round, clapping her hands together. "Let's explore the castle some more, shall we?"

"I'm going to draw some of those carvings," announced Theo. "Some of them are fantastic, especially the lions and dragons, and those smiling faces are wonderful on the fireplace. Who do you think the two 'C's are for? Maybe his children, or for him and his wife?"

Theo got his notepad and a pencil, and sucking one end thoughtfully he paced around, looking at the immense beams and intricate detailed carvings. Arabella helped him choose the very special ones and together they became engrossed in the duke's wonderful and imaginary world. Theo reached the hallway where the mythical beasts were to be found carved into the stair bannisters, and the posts at the bottom where two toads with wings and bulging eyes kept guard; their webbed feet were balanced on a lily pad and the flowers of the water lily entwined around the post.

Theo sketched madly, trying to get it just right. He moved on to a panel with a lion, his shaggy head standing out from his body, which had six legs. Instinctively Theo reached out to stroke its head, and it felt just a little wobbly.

"Oh, this is loose, Bella."

She came to look at it and stroked it too.

"It's not quite straight, is it?" and she gave it a twist. "That's better."

Theo heard a faint noise and with an eerie creak the panel with the lion on it opened.

"What have you done, Bella?" Theo called out in alarm, as the panel swung open completely and stopped.

"It's not falling off, stupid, it's a door!" Bella said firmly. "I didn't do anything! Look, it's got hinges here."

They examined the door and wrenched it open. Inside was a dark square cupboard with nothing inside at all; dust and cobwebs clung to the edges.

"But what's it for?" said Theo. "It doesn't go anywhere."

"Is it hollow at the back?"

They tapped the walls. They did sound hollow and echoey but there were no handles or levers or any way to open them.

"It's just a glorified broom cupboard," decided Theo, disappointed, and he twisted the lion back to close the door.

He moved on to the dragon who faced the lion, wings spread upwards and tail curved downwards. It was fantastic, with large scales on his body and big clawed feet. Arabella tried twisting and pushing all the large features but nothing happened. They were both bitterly disappointed so they turned and faced the doorway opposite which had a long snake wreathed around the frame; his head and tongue hung outwards over the door. Theo sighed, he was getting tired and frustrated and leaned his back against the staircase to look upwards at the snake. The eyes of the snake seemed to be very bright and highly polished. Suddenly the sun came out and it seemed to light up the snake's eyes. Theo gasped in fright and tumbled backwards, hitting his back on the dragon's large feet. Arabella caught him. A horrible grating noise came from the panels, and the twins clung to each other.

"What's that?" Theo whispered, but Arabella wasn't easily scared.

"It's behind that panel," she said firmly. "Open it again, Theo, something's going on in there."

He twisted the lion's head again and the panel unlatched itself and swung outwards. A set of stairs revealed themselves. A floor had slid across, which explained the grating noise.

"A secret room! Lots of castles have them. I bet you this staircase goes to a secret room," said Theo, almost too excited to speak.

"It's very dark." Bella hesitated, she didn't really like the dark much.

"Come on, we've got to go down. We'll be very careful and feel each step before we stand on it. Let's get a stick each, I'll be braver then. It'll be alright, Bella."

He persisted, trying to win her approval. Armed with a walking stick each from the large stand in the hall, they began their perilous descent. It was rather cobwebby, which was horrible in the dark, but steadily they went down until they reached the bottom where daylight helped them. The secret room had one small window, just a little square. A ledge and a stone with a handle drilled into it were a clue.

"This fits the window Theo, it must do," and Arabella tried it. It was perfect.

"Must be a spy hole, because hardly any light comes in."

On one of the shelves were some candles and a tinder box.

"Perfect, we can have some more light."

Their fascination with history and lots of visits to other castles meant they really did know how things were done in the old days. The tinder box contained a flint, a bar and some fine straw. Striking the flint against the bar made sparks to ignite the straw. If they were very lucky, they might be able to light the candles. Bella had seen it done at an exhibition. Theo, however, was the one who finally set the straw alight in the box, and then held the candles into the small flame. How much better it felt with some light! They noticed everything, then – the fireplace, sink, shelves, bed – it was the perfect hideaway.

"Let's move down here," suggested Bella, "it's much cosier and we've got a fire."

"But what about going home? How will Mum and Dad find us?" Theo was getting anxious.

"We'll go back on the last day, then Mum and Dad will be coming to fetch us. It serves Auntie Edna and Uncle Arnold right. They shouldn't have been so horrid to us, should they?"

Bella was quite determined, Theo could see that.

"Okay, okay," he conceded.

"Right, let's get this place sorted."

They got to work immediately to re-arrange the secret room. As the supplies and their belongings were being bumped down the stairs, Bella knocked against something, which caused the floor to grate and slide noisily closed with a clunk and a grind.

"Oh no, it's closed up!" and she grabbed

Theo's arm. "What shall we do? Will we get it open again?"

"Of course we will, the duke must have got back upstairs again, mustn't he?"

Suddenly they didn't feel quite so happy at the thought of being closed up in the secret room, and to make things worse they couldn't find any way to get the floor, now their ceiling, open again. Arabella thought hard about what to do. They drank a bottle of green lemonade between them and Theo, staring into the empty glass, had a brainwave.

"Put a message in the bottle and throw it out of the spyhole! Somebody will find it."

"Yes! And it can't go anywhere else but around the lake."

Theo tore a page from his notebook and wrote the message.

*STUCK IN A SECRET ROOM BELOW THE CASTLE OF CHARLEMAGNE. WED MAY 3RD. THEO AND BELLA GLUM. HELP US PLEASE.*

"Is that alright?"

"That's great."

And they put the screw top on and unceremoniously lobbed it through the small opening. It splashed into the water.

"Can you see it?" Bella climbed onto a chair for a better look. She watched it in silence until it disappeared.

"Good luck, little bottle," she whispered, and gave an impish smile to Theo. "That will do the trick, don't worry."

What Arabella and Theo didn't know was that underneath the worn Persian carpet was a trap door which led to the lake, but even if they had found it, they didn't have a boat and it was a very long way to swim. But help was to come from an unexpected source…

# Chapter 14

# Two lost children

Those lemonade bottles of Mrs Magill's were not ordinary bottles, as we already know, and that bottle took on a life of its own. Like a torpedo it sped through the water back to Goodly Harbour, leaving a small wake behind it. It reached the slipway at Eight Bells Cottage and in no time at all bounced up the cobbles, standing itself upright just outside

Mr Noodlenutt's doorway and next to Mrs Magill's shop. It rocked backwards and forwards, making a loud tinkling glassy sort of noise, like a bottle rolling down a street; someone was bound to hear it very soon.

Back at Haven's Rest, in Little Rushing, the Glums really weren't too bothered about the disappearance of Theo and Arabella. They had woken up stiff and sore from their painful experiences and reluctantly gone about their work as usual.

"I expect those dreadful children are playing somewhere. That's what children do, isn't it?"

"Yes, dear. They don't like washing themselves or helping in the house, do they? I'm surprised so many people have children, they are nothing but a nuisance really."

The Glums moaned on and on. What this unkind couple didn't know was that Reginald and Annie May had rung several times to speak to their children. Not receiving an answer, they cancelled their plans at once and headed by car to Goodly Harbour, fearing something terrible had happened. They were driving down the motorway and would be at the cottage by nightfall.

Mr Noodlenutt, disturbed by the clanking and clinking of the bottle dancing a jig on the cobbles, came out to see what it was. He picked up the bottle and opened the top, then he pulled out the folded piece of paper. After reading it he was very concerned. He went at once to Mrs Magill's shop.

"One of yours I believe, Mrs Magill."

She was standing as usual, calm and smiling, behind her counter.

"Why, yes it is, those two children bought two bottles only the other day, and a few pastries."

"Well, it seems they're in trouble, look at this," and he offered her the note.

"Escaped from their persecutors I expect, poor little dears. They'll be alright I'm sure, quite a resourceful pair I'd imagine, and I think they have adequate provisions. Do you know anything about this secret room?"

"Nobody knows anything about the Castle of Charlemagne. You've got to look very hard to find it."

"You've got thermal imaging in Crocco, haven't you? Cutting equipment? Abseiling ropes?"

"Of course," replied Mr Noodlenutt, surprised at her knowledge.

"I know you'll find them," she said, and after washing the lemonade bottle she replaced it on the very top of the pyramid of green glass bottles in the corner. Promptly it turned green and filled itself up with fizzy bubbles of lemonade.

"You know where you've been, little green bottle, don't you? You can go into Crocco's tank then, and it should all be so easy." Satisfaction spread all over her face. She did like to help in her own little ways.

By the time it was dark there were quite a few different things going on, and not all of them were pleasant. Edna and Annie May Glum were sisters-in-law but if you had heard them screaming at each other you would have thought they were the bitterest of enemies.

"Where are my beautiful children? How dare you lose them!"

"They are dreadful children and they

have lost themselves!"

"Where did you see them last?"

"They've been hiding for several days, naughty, disobedient little wretches!"

Annie May was bright red with rage and went to slap Edna Glum's face, when suddenly the old nasty fell on the floor with terrible pains in her legs. Then she clutched her chest with both hands and promptly fainted.

Her husband looked worried. "Oh dear, I do hope—"

Arnold was cut short in his speaking as pains shot all over his arms and chest and head, and he too sank to the floor and passed out cold.

"Jolly good. Just what you deserve," sniffed Annie May, and stepped over the two people lying side by side on the flagstone floor.

"My dear, that is rather harsh," snapped Reginald, who did not like disagreements, or the look of the two people lying motionless.

"What? Don't you care about our dear, dear, boy and girl? I'm off to the nearest police station, the children must be found, and *they*—" pointing to the floor, "—will be arrested! I never want to see them again as long as I live!"

Annie May dragged Reginald after her and proceeded to the train, which would take her across the lake to Goodly Harbour police station.

Bella and Theo were finishing off the two gingerbread people, as I expect you guessed. Arm by arm, leg by leg, followed by body and head, they crunched, chewed and swallowed the biscuits they had so kindly bought for their auntie and uncle. Somehow, Mrs Magill's magic had worked in its mysterious way.

"Let's light the fire," said Arabella. "We'll have to use those old logs stacked in the corner. I'll make some pancakes with the flour and eggs."

Theo agreed, and using the tinderbox once more he managed to ignite some pieces of torn sacking which he had patiently shredded into fine threads. Gradually the fire increased, until Arabella could balance a flat griddle on it. In another shallow pan she boiled some water from the well. The pancakes were not too bad and the green lemonade bottle filled itself up again as soon as it was empty. The flour in the packet seemed to stay pretty full, so they were not worried about starving. As the fire grew brighter, smoke streamed out of the chimney into the air above the castle.

Col Boodle-Smith saw the smoke again. He was at the boring stage of rubbing down poor old *Duty*, which had been retrieved from the lake and repaired, and any distraction was welcome. He frowned. "Something's up along the lake, not squatters I hope. Hmm, maybe I should investigate. Yes, I think I will."

He dressed himself in his old combat gear, took a torch and a knife, and climbed through his garden into the steep forest behind his house. He shouted to his wife loudly, "Off on a recce, Queenie dear, smoke in the forest. Don't worry about me!"

"I won't, dear!" she called back, and turned the television on to her favourite programme, opened a new box of chocolates and settled down.

"He'll be gone for hours!" she thought gleefully.

Mr Noodlenutt and Crocco were preparing for a search up the river, checking the equipment and refilling the fuel tank with a bottle of green lemonade particularly chosen by Mrs Magill.

"This will help."

She smiled, handing him two extra, spares for the children she knew he would be bringing back.

Meanwhile, Sgt Huff was trying to keep the irate and distraught parents calm. Mr and Mrs Reginald Glum had found their saviour and he was not getting away now. Sgt Huff got out a new notebook and started taking notes.

"Have you got a photo of them, please?" he asked, and Annie May produced several out of her handbag.

"I'll get some posters made up for missing persons. Now, give me the details."

Calling her children "missing persons" was the last straw for Annie May and she collapsed in tears, sobbing loudly.

"Now, now, that won't help," soothed Sgt Huff awkwardly, and Reginald tried to comfort her.

"It's all your fault," she sobbed, shaking off his arm. "You and your banking conference in Brighton. If we hadn't gone, this would never have happened!"

Mrs Huff appeared, and glaring at the two men, she put her arm around Annie May and led her gently upstairs for a cup of tea.

"Leave it to me!" she hissed at her husband. "Let him help you!" and she nodded at the unfortunate Reginald. "Come along, my dear," and she ushered Annie away.

Within an hour, the news had gone around the small town about the two missing children. Everybody who had seem them offered a snippet of information, until a short history of their actions over the last few days could be put together. Their photos appeared in a poster promptly printed out at the police station and circulated around the shops and houses. Dr Proctor remembered seeing them in the railway yard and he phoned Mr Noodlenutt to tell him.

News had not yet reached the hydro-electric station, or Sparky Watts and Bill Brightly could have been of great help.

As it was, dear old Col Boodle-Smith was the first person to reach the Castle of Charlemagne. He found the steps which the children had uncovered. Then he crept around the battlements and saw the smoke coming out of the chimney. Unfortunately, he could not squeeze his large person through the broken bars of the casement window.

"Maybe someone entered the castle from the rocks on the lakeside," he thought, as there was no other way to reach the main entrance.

At one of his old appointed times, he decided to signal a short message to Sgt Huff, just in case. It was, after all, his duty to report the smoke.

He trudged back home, feeling rather tired, to find Queenie asleep, the chocolate box empty and no lunch. He went to his summerhouse by the lake to send his Morse code message, giving his own call sign first, but there was no answer. Sgt Huff was too busy.

"Never mind, I have done my duty."

Then, remembering the tiny rubber dingy Queenie had bought him for his birthday, he had an idea. He could explore the castle from the lake after all. After pumping it up, he was ready to go. "I'll send one more signal to Sgt Huff just in case."

He really was trying to be responsible and make amends for his previous mistakes.

This time, Sgt Huff was eating a toasted sandwich in his office. The interview with the Glums had exhausted him and at last they had left. His wife had handled Annie May beautifully, and everyone was hopeful for a swift recovery of the twins.

The flashing light caught Sgt Huff by surprise. He looked at his watch. It must be something important as he hadn't heard from that old coot for a long time. Grabbing his own torch, he gave his call sign back. Then he read this message,

SMOKE AT CASTLE OF CHARLEMAGNE. INVESTIGATING.

"Hmm, maybe that old duffer's onto something. I'll get out the police launch. Better reply first," and he sent a message back.

OK. JOIN YOU LATER.

Sgt Huff called his wife loudly.

"Can you help me this afternoon, my dear?

227

Number three uniform and waterproofs, please."

Mrs Huff put her head around the door.

"Part-time pay this time, Otto? You did promise."

"Yes, yes alright, I'll put in an official claim when we get back."

"Then I will."

Ten minutes later they were ready and untying the launch.

"We'll handle this missing person's inquiry ourselves. Got the check list?"

He reeled it off at amazing speed. "Oars, spare batteries, flares, rope, ship-to-shore radio, flask of chocolate, blankets, whistle, torch, lifejackets. Okay? Good to go?" and they chugged off up the lake to investigate.

Of course, by now at the castle the fire had died down, red embers glowed brightly and no smoke was visible. Bella and Theo were fast asleep, full of pancakes and green lemonade, tucked up under the large heavy damask curtain.

The older Glums, at Haven's Rest, had taken themselves off to bed after waking up exhausted with aches and pains and a headache. Poor old Derek was manning the office again. He pulled his hat and jacket on and opened a new packet of wine gums; this could be a long afternoon.

Reginald and Annie May Glum had booked into the Lakeside View Hotel and ordered tea and cake in their room. A waiter brought the tray in. Two pretty strawberry tarts lay on a lace doily, alongside a small tin of shortbread with a picture of a castle on the front.

"Compliments of the house, sir, madam," and the boy smiled kindly. "Mrs Magill's cakes are the best in town. We'll hope for good news soon." He quietly left the room.

The cakes did look very enticing on the plate, and even though the Glums were very tired and sick with worry, the strawberry tarts with their glazed topping, crisp shell and swirl of piped cream, seemed to be begging to be eaten; the mint leaf and chocolate cherry did the trick.

"Can't waste these, dear, try one with a cup of tea," coaxed Reginald, and as he poured out the fragrant tea, Annie May sighed and agreed.

They ate in silence, gazing out of the window and then at the tin of shortbread with the castle on the lid. They both felt very tired. Reginald opened the bedroom door and hung the DO NOT DISTURB sign on the handle.

"I think we should have a nap, my dear, while we wait for news. It will do us good." He patted his wife's hand gently. "Come along."

Without a word they climbed onto the big soft bed, and within a few seconds they were both fast asleep.

Sgt Huff and Nora his wife slowly scanned the edge of the lake with binoculars, until Nora was sure she had found the castle. It was very well hidden, obscured with years and years of brambles and sapling trees. As they ventured up the narrow rocky inlet, Sgt Huff spied a small tender tied up at the remains of the wooden jetty.

"Boodle-Smith's here, look. I had a signal from him earlier," and he sniffed in a rather pompous way.

Tying up at the rickety jetty, they carefully went ashore, torch and whistle at the ready. The big old door with all the black rusting studs was firmly closed. Sgt Huff tied a rope around his waist and squeezed around the side of the castle where it was wet and rocky. Several large brambles had been hacked down.

"Boodle-Smith must have come this way. Follow me, Nora, and hold onto the rope."

Nora, who was a great walker and very fit, easily followed. Eventually they reached the first floor with the other door and the barred casement window. Col Boodle-Smith was sitting rather ungracefully against the wall, puffing. He was red in the face and mopping himself with a large spotted handkerchief.

"Good morning, sergeant. Quite a climb. Can't get in. Don't hear anything. Smoke's gone. What to do, eh?" His words came in short gasps.

Sgt Huff examined the bars. "Two of these have been broken off recently, look." He pointed to the rusty flakes on the ground.

"Can't get through there," gasped the colonel. "Not in a million years."

"No, but Nora can."

Sgt Huff indicated to his wife that she should climb through the gap.

"Here's a whistle, dear, you'll be alright, off you go." He pointed to the window and nodded. "Don't touch anything will you? Do you want my notebook to jot down your observations?" and he fished in the top pocket of his uniform.

Nora just gave him one of her looks and he stopped trying to get the notebook out.

"Perhaps not, then."

Nimbly, Nora placed one arm and one leg astride the stone casement and squeezed through the gap. She disappeared into the darkness. Then the torch light's beam could be seen flickering around.

"Anything?" called Sgt Huff, peering behind her.

"Can't see much, it's rather dark in here…" Her voice got fainter and fainter and then it was quiet.

Nora opened some of the bedroom doors, as the children had done before her and she too marvelled at the preserved state of the rooms and its furniture. No signs of anybody. As her eyes accustomed to the gloom she saw the staircase and all the incredible carvings. She was amazed and intrigued. Reaching the large hallway, the dining room, living room and kitchen, there were still no signs of life. She did go to the fireplace and saw the ash, but as she pushed her finger gently into the grey pile, it felt cold. One of the curtains was missing but it hadn't fallen off the pole or lay in a heap on the floor. There really was no sign of anyone or anything. Then something caught her eye; in the corner of the fireplace was a screwed-up piece of paper with a blue pattern on it. She unwrapped it with interest. It was two oval greaseproof cake papers from Mrs Magill's shop.

"How interesting! Somebody has been eating cakes in here. How romantic, beside the fire." She imagined two people meeting here, sharing cakes and declaring their love for each other. Perhaps two young people, or even two old people? They must be thin," she smiled to herself, "or they couldn't get in! I'm not going to show this to Otto. It could just ruin a beautiful love affair." And she pushed the papers into her pocket. Nora took one last look around the lonely old castle and tried to imagine it full of life and colour, blazing fires, candlelight, laughter and well-dressed people in satins and silks. She sighed; how splendid it must have been! Quickly she returned to her husband and the colonel, who were waiting impatiently for news.

She appeared from the stone casement, shaking her head. "Nothing. Nobody. Not a clue or a sound. Sorry, dear," and she secretly added up how much this enjoyable 'work' had earned her: Otto would have to pay her for her time – marvellous!

"Where *did* that smoke come from, then?" persisted Col Boodle-Smith.

"Picnickers in the woods. Just looked like it came from here," insisted Sgt Huff. Both men were unhappy with the lack of results, especially as there were no children to return to their anxious parents.

"Is there anywhere else they could have got to? The hydro-electric station or the windmill? They could have walked up there," suggested Nora.

"I suppose it's possible, we'd better try them," agreed Sgt Huff. "You can go now," he nodded to the colonel, "and thanks anyway," he added gruffly.

Col Boodle-Smith was bitterly disappointed and began to untie his boat. He only just fitted into the little rubber tender, which wobbled and swayed dangerously when he got into it. He roared off and in no time was back home telling Queenie all about it.

"Children can't just disappear, Archibald," she told him wisely. "Either they're stuck somewhere or they've been kidnapped. Has anyone checked that they haven't just gone home? Who could blame them anyway?" she added with feeling.

Col Boodle-Smith poured himself a large brandy and sat dejectedly, thinking hard. He had so wanted to do something truly heroic for a change.

Theo and Arabella woke up several hours later and removed the stone from the spyhole. They took it in turns to peer out. There were no boats to see, the lake was quite empty. No rescuers yet.

Sadly, when Mr and Mrs Huff got to the hydro-electric station, Sparky and Bill had gone down to Goodly Harbour for supplies, and Dusty Dave the miller knew nothing about anything. The police launch returned to its mooring and Sgt Huff sat by his telephone waiting for something to happen. It was a proper mystery.

Col Boodle-Smith returned to the very boring task of rubbing his boat down, when Bill and Sparky came past in their pilot boat.

"You haven't seen two kids have you, by any chance?" he shouted out, so they brought their boat alongside.

"We heard the news in the town. Yes, we did see them a couple of days ago. A boy and a girl, just like the posters. They left us to look for the Castle of Charlemagne. We told them it was hereabouts. Poor young folks was staying with the Glums. Can you imagine?"

"It seems they've just vanished, there's been a right to-do. Parents are here trying to locate them. I've been up to the castle with Sgt Huff but there's no sign of them," the colonel told them.

"We'll keep an eye out. I did see some smoke a while back," said Bill thoughtfully, "down in that direction." And he pointed.

"So did I!" agreed the colonel in excitement.

"Be in touch then," and the two men turned the pilot boat towards the head of the lake.

The colonel watched them go, staring after them until they disappeared in the far distance. He was thinking all the time. So they had seen the smoke too. Then another thought came to him: what if the children didn't want to be found? What if they had hidden on purpose to get away from the Glums? They wouldn't have wanted Nora Huff to find them and could have hidden away until she'd gone. He must watch again for the smoke; and this time, the colonel was on the right track.

Dr Proctor joined Mr Noodlenutt and Crocco at 4 p.m. exactly, after the last train had crossed the bridge. They set off up the lake with ancient maps and old charts which marked the Castle of Charlemagne, and of course, they had the help of the green lemonade. Not wanting to attract the attention of either the harbour master or Sgt Huff they proceeded to dive below the water and set a course for their proposed location. Only the thin black pipe was visible, travelling slowly up the lake.

The two men were devising their plan; every word of Theo's note was examined in detail.

'Stuck'… meant they couldn't get out, but somehow they had got in. An entrance was evident somewhere. 'Below the castle' implied just that, somewhere under the castle, maybe in a part that could not be seen. 'Secret room' was the most difficult one because it had been excavated purposely to be unnoticed and unable to be accessed by ordinary means, i.e. stairs or doors. This was going to be the hardest secret to break.

Mr Noodlenutt let the underwater car drive himself on the autopilot. The green lemonade had been there before and was giving out signals on the screen which matched one of the old parchment maps from the museum that Dr Proctor had 'borrowed'. They arrived at the front of the inlet and Mr Noodlenutt got out his thermal imaging equipment and scanned the castle. Low down, beneath the windowless walls, he could see the shapes of two people on the screen. "Look! There they are! Under the castle! There has to be a way out from below otherwise there was no point building it."

"I agree, better get your diving gear on, Noodlenutt, go exploring!"

So Mr Noodlenutt, kitted up in helmet, suit, and boots, took a torch and a knife and crept out of Crocco's special watertight chamber. It was very rocky and he stumbled a few times. Dr Proctor, manning the air pump held his breath – he didn't want the air hose to get kinked up.

With his torch, Mr Noodlenutt examined the foundations of the castle. He noticed the old stone jetty cut into the rocky cliffs, and a stone flight of steps leading to a wooden trap door only inches above the water. He made his way up there tapped on the door with his heavy torch…

# Chapter 15

# Crocco goes searching

Annie May dreamed of her children: they were running and laughing, playing hide and seek, dressed in old-fashioned white pinafores and trousers. Round and round they ran, making her dizzy; down the narrow spiral steps, peeping out of every window on their way down the old tower, and waving their handkerchiefs from some old stone walls. She could see Bella's red knitted beret; she waved back.

Annie May woke up with a jump, and for a minute, her heart beating fast, she didn't know where she was. Gradually everything came back to her, but she didn't feel sad. She felt happy and excited. Reginald was fast asleep, and she slipped out of bed and walked towards the window. She passed the tin of shortbread on the tray, and glancing at the picture of the lovely castle, she saw something move; high on the turret were Bella and Theo waving to her. Dressed in white, Bella had her red beret on. Tiny, tiny figures moving, smiling and waving on the top of the tin.

Annie May fainted on the floor. At once, Reginald jumped out of bed to help her. As she regained consciousness, she smiled. "I know where they are. I've seen them. At the castle, the one on the tin."

At once, Reginald phoned the doctor, fearing the worst, and then he ordered some tea. He was very worried about his wife but she seemed so happy and still talking about a castle. Reginald thought it had been too much for her and she'd lost her mind.

Col. Boodle-Smith didn't waste time with his boat. He crept back along the forest path behind his house, a rucksack strapped to his back. He had done some deep thinking and had some new ideas to try out. He reached the second level and opened his bag. He took out a hand-held electric drill with a cutting disc on it and with determination cut through all the remaining rusty bars of the casement window. The bars fell off one by one.

"Gotcha!"

He was very satisfied, now he could get in. Repacking his tools, he threw the bag into the open window and followed it. Out came the powerful torch in his pocket and he too found himself in the wonderful carved world of the old duke.

Searching the bedrooms held fast in time, he admired the furniture, tapestries and paintings, arriving at the staircase, hall

and living rooms, as he explored further –
all silent as the grave.

He knew that long ago, during wars
and conflicts, soldiers, priests, princes and
kings had been hidden in old country
houses and castles. Why, during the last war,
escaped prisonerhad been hidden by the
French, waiting for a chance to get back to
England. His mind was set. Somewhere in
this castle the children were hidden and he
was going to find them. Priest holes, secret
doors and sliding panels were common in
these places. He surveyed the rooms looking
for likely spots; wooden walls and stone
fireplaces. The carved animals, birds and
reptiles all watched him. Eyes followed him
round as he searched. He tapped in different
area with a small mallet, searching,
searching, and listening for hollow sounds.
He returned again to the staircase in the
hall. The lion and the dragon stared stonily
at him, and looking up he could almost hear
the snake hissing, its protruding tongue
pointing across the corridor and its polished
eyes glittering at him.

Col Boodle-Smith turned around and tapped the wooden panel by the lion. It was definitely hollow. He felt hot and excited. How did it open? He felt all along the edges, then kneeling down, tapped along the floor. It was the right sound. He heaved his big bulky frame up by holding on to the protruding head of the lion, and as it twisted in his outstretched hand, he toppled over onto the floor… but as he sat up, he saw the panel open: he had twisted the secret latch! At once he scrambled to his feet to look inside. It was completely empty.

"It can't be empty!"

He refused to believe it. So near! He'd been right all along and knew these old mechanisms were often cunningly installed. Nothing could be too easy or there would be no point hiding; not if someone wanted to kill you. He pushed and pulled, twisted and pressed everything he could see. Every mythical creature was tested but nothing happened. He slid down the wall in frustration and sat on the floor, weary and cross. He was so close. It was extremely annoying. "Something else happens in that cupboard, it's got to," he told himself, "Now think, Archibald, think!"

Col Boodle-Smith might be an old duffer now, but he didn't get to be a colonel in the British Army by giving up. He banged his head against the stairs as he racked his brains for inspiration. "Ouch! That hurt." And as he rubbed his head a grinding, grating sound reached his ears. "Oh my hat, that's it!"

He sprang to his feet, bruised head forgotten, as he saw the floor disappearing into the wall and the staircase was revealed.

"Jumping Jehoshaphat, a secret staircase!" and he roared with excited laughter. "You've done it, Archie, you've done it! Now, keep calm, get your tools and prop that door open," he decided wisely. "Don't want to get stuck down there, do I?" So he placed a chisel under the cupboard door to wedge it before switching on his torch, putting his backpack on and very warily placing his foot on the first tread of the stairs. What would he find? He wasn't quite sure…

# Reunited

Back at Haven's Rest, Mr and Mrs Glum opened their eyes slowly. The sun was trying to shine in through the dusty window pane, and a bird was singing joyfully in the trees.

"Arnold?" whispered Mrs Glum.

"Yes, Edna?" Mr Glum whispered back.

"We're not dead and gone to heaven, are we?"

"No dear, I don't think we're dead," reassured Mr Glum.

"That's alright then."

Mrs Glum leapt out of bed in her dark brown pyjamas and climbed onto a chair to reach the top of the wardrobe. She pulled an old crocodile-skin suitcase down and it tumbled onto the floor.

"What are you doing, dear?" asked Arnold.

"Well, if we're not dead, I'm feeling very much alive and glad I am of it too!" she told him joyfully. Opening the suitcase, she beamed at the contents – it was full of £20 notes.

"It's time we enjoyed our life a bit. Let's spend it all! After all, it wouldn't be any use to us if we had woken up dead, would it?"

Arnold didn't quite understand her line of thinking. Mrs Glum then ran downstairs to the telephone. She looked up the number of Adam and Eve's hairdressers and made two appointments for later. Then she rang the travel agents, Sea and Shore, and booked a cruise to the Greek islands for the following month. Next, she lit the fire and burnt all their clothes, except the ones hanging on the end of the bed.

"Come on, get dressed!" she scolded Arnold. "We're going shopping."

Within half an hour they were in Hartfield's Country Store in the village, buying everything new from top to toe. They only just made the hairdressers' in time.

"Morning Mr Glum, morning Mrs Glum," said Olive politely. "Just a dry trim for both of you? A quarter of an inch?"

"No, no, I want a restyle today and I'm going blonde," announced Mrs Glum.

"It's quite expensive," apologised the surprised assistant.

"Oh, I don't mind," said Edna cheerily, "what's money for if not to spend?"

Within two hours Arnold and Edna Glum were totally unrecognisable. In fact, they both looked quite nice.

"Here you are," Edna beamed, and gave Olive a large tip.

Olive didn't know what to think. What had happened to the Glums? Had they won the Lottery? It seemed likely. "Thank you" seemed the best option.

"Well, we'd better try and track down Reggie and Annie May. I'm sure they must have found those nice children by now. Shall we, dear?" asked Mrs Glum, patting her blonde styled hair.

"Whatever you say," said a very smart-looking Arnold. "What about Derek?"

"Oh yes, Derek. He must be due for some pay by now. How long has he been working for us?"

"Five years, dear."

"He's entitled to a little bonus then, for long service."

"I think so," agreed Mr Glum.

So they went to see the long-suffering, kindly Derek. He was stunned. Not only were the Glums not looking a bit like the Glums he was used to, but they offered him money as well. He was speechless, and choked on a green wine gum.

"There, there." Mr Glum patted him on the back. "We won't be long, Derek old man."

And off they went, leaving the

bewildered Derek behind to look after the ticket office once again.

Reginald and Annie May burst into Sgt Huff's office.

"I know where they are! They're in a castle!" She beamed at the surprised man.

"Really? We have already organised a thorough search of the entire area, Mrs Glum, and it did include the Castle of Charlemagne. My personal assistant has looked inside the building with all due diligence, sadly to no avail." He folded his hands and laid them on the desk. "I am, of course, open to new thoughts and lines of inquiry if you have any." He looked at them both with a serious expression.

"But they are there, I know they are, I saw them clearly on the biscuit tin lid!"

Reginald and Sgt Huff's eyes met.

"My wife has just seen Dr Kickletoff and he has given her a special tablet, sergeant." Reginald winked at the stern face of Sgt Huff, who cleared his throat and looked away.

"Ahhh, hmm. Let us consider all this

carefully, Mr and Mrs Glum. We cannot waste manpower on whims and fancies, we must have facts. Facts are what the police deal in. Now—"

He looked up, but Annie May had disappeared. She had run off down to the lakeside to hire a boat. She knew she was right. Nothing would stop her.

Sgt Huff and her husband stared at each other uncomfortably. This was going to be tricky. Reginald was torn between sound logic and his belief in his wife's good sense. What should he do?

"I must go with her sergeant, you understand, I'm sure. If nothing else it gives us something to do."

"Go, yes go and I wish you good luck," Sgt Huff told him as he hurried out to follow Annie. "I'm sure they will be found soon, everyone is looking for them."

Everyone was, and at that moment, Theo and Arabella were listening in horror to the knocking under the floor and the sound of heavy footsteps coming upwards, getting closer. Clutching onto each other, they closed their eyes and waited. From under the old Persian rug an ancient wooden trap door creaked slowly open. Theo opened one eye; a copper diving helmet emerged through the opening. Mr Noodlenutt could not, however, climb the rest of the steps without the buoyancy of the water to help him. His boots were just too heavy. His face smiled at Theo from behind the glass window of his helmet.

Then Col Boodle-Smith arrived from the secret staircase he had discovered and saw the children standing together, looking rather frightened.

"I knew it! I've found you! I'm rather chuffed with myself, I must say! Ah, Noodlenutt… you're here too. I say, a trap door!" His eyes widened in surprise. "How very interesting, an exit route obviously."

Mr Noodlenutt sat on the edge of the floor and took off his helmet. He shook out his grey corkscrew curls and smiled at the two nervous children.

"You must be Theo and Arabella. How do you do? How clever of you to find this secret room."

The children unfroze a little and smiled back. Arabella nudged her brother.

"Oh yes, how do you do," stammered Theo, politely offering to shake hands.

The colonel strode into the room and patted them both on the back,

"And I am Colonel Boodle-Smith. Had a devil of a job to get down here, quite a mystery, but… well, here we are!" and he grinned from ear to ear.

"Well, Noodlenutt, how did you find them? How did you know about the trap door?"

Before anyone could answer, Dr Proctor's head appeared from the open hatchway.

"Hello everyone, I've brought Crocco alongside. Not much headroom Noodlenutt, but ready and waiting. You must be Theo and Arabella, what an interesting castle this is. I'd love to see around!"

And so before anyone knew it, Theo, Arabella, Col Boodle-Smith and Dr Proctor had gone off on a guided tour.

"Well!" said Mr Noodlenutt, a bit

disappointed. "I can't go anywhere in these boots," and he sat waiting for their return.

In a little while, an engine could be heard chugging nearby and getting louder. The eagle eyes of Annie May had spotted the castle, and coming in closer to investigate she had seen Crocco bobbing under the jetty.

"Whatever's that?" She pointed. "It looks like a huge crocodile!"

Reginald wasn't keen to go any further. "Maybe we shouldn't get too close."

"Nonsense! We're here now, come on it won't eat you!"

It was clear where Arabella got her stubborn, adventurous nature from. As the boat motored gently towards the lower walls of the castle, both people could make out the stone steps carved into the small standing jetty.

"It's an underground entrance, I'm sure of it, and that crocodile seems to have an engine running." Reginald was getting excited.

With that, Mr Noodlenutt came down the steps very clumsily and looked out over the lake. He saw two people and waved.

"Ahoy there! Not looking for Theo and Arabella are you, by any chance?" he called with a chuckle.

"Yes!" shouted Annie May, "We are!"

"Well, you've come to the right place. They're here, in fact I think you're just in time for pancakes!"

When her parents arrived, Arabella was showing off her cooking skills and Theo demonstrating the fire and the workings of a mediaeval castle kitchen.

"At last! We've been so worried about you!" and great hugs were exchanged.

"Look, Mum, this is all so wonderful." Theo untangled himself from his parents to show them the well, the chimney, and he opened the bread oven to show Dr Proctor. Several other cubby holes looked rather interesting.

"What's this?" the doctor asked, pointing.

"Don't know," shrugged Theo, "I haven't looked up there."

Dr Proctor, who was very tall, reached up and twisted one of the latches, opened the small door, and gingerly put his fingers inside. He could feel something large in there. Stretching up on his toes, he put in both hands and pulled out a small metal casket. The entwined metal 'C's and coronet were incised on it.

"What have we here?" It was all very exciting.

"Those are the same initials that are on the fireplace upstairs," Theo said at once.

"We can research that later. It could hold some clues about this whole fascinating place." Dr Proctor smiled. "Would you like me to take charge of it?"

"We'd all be very grateful," replied Reginald.

The seven assorted people squeezed together around the table in the secret room and ate pancake after pancake. Arabella really did have the knack for them and the flour never seemed to run out. When they were all truly full up, Reginald and Annie May thanked everyone who had helped to find their children. Col Boodle-Smith beamed with pleasure and was lost for words.

"Perhaps we can discuss our family affairs later, children," said their father very meaningfully, looking hard at his son and daughter.

"Yes, Dad." Theo and Arabella both nodded, knowing quite well they were in for a good telling-off. Both tried to think of plenty of excuses.

"I'll close up the castle if you want to go off with your Mum and Dad," offered the colonel kindly. "I've left my things upstairs."

"Thank you, colonel."

Reginald helped the children to collect up their belongings and guided them down through the opening, to the low steps and their waiting boat.

"And thank you, gentlemen," turning to Mr Noodlenutt and Dr Proctor.

"Our pleasure." They both bowed.

Off went the young Glum family. Theo and Arabella gazed longingly back at their castle. They had to admit it was very nice to be together again at last.

"Fascinating place," remarked Dr Proctor, "all that wonderful carving, and that mechanism for the secret room, all very clever. It ought to be open to the public. It's a masterpiece."

"You're right," agreed the colonel. "Perhaps if you track down the owners it could be bought by the town? It's a great attraction, indeed. Indeed." He started thinking again.

"We must be off," Mr Noodlenutt smiled. "All's well that ends well, colonel. Very well done," and he and Dr Proctor left to go back to an impatient Crocco; he had missed all the fun.

The colonel closed the trap door, replaced the old Persian rug, tidied up the kitchen army-style, went up the secret stairs and entered the small cupboard to look for a way to close the staircase from the inside. He examined everything with his torch. He knew now that the lion opened the panel, and the dragon's foot operated the sliding floor, but closing it from the inside was still a mystery. Then he noticed a small carved mouse. It looked as if it was running up to the top if the staircase.

Nothing else was nearby – it was the only animal inside the secret compartment, so it had to be the secret lever! The colonel took hold of it and it slid forward on a little metal groove. The grinding started, and he had to be careful of his head. He smiled to himself.

"Gotcha!"

He was delighted with himself. He slid the little mouse back the other way and the staircase opened again. Marvellous! Standing outside the secret room and looking at the panel's wonderful carvings he saw something else. Tucked up behind the dragon's tail was a small mouse; it must have been the clue nobody had noticed, because it was exactly the same as the one inside. Then he saw another one, in front of the dragon's foot. "Ah ha! This is very clever! These mice have got their eyes closed. Three blind mice! Of course! Only two here, the third is down below on the stairs. Well I'm blowed!" He was delighted. "Three blind mice, eh? Who would have thought it!" he chuckled, thrilled and excited to have made his own discovery. "That duke was quite something. I'd like to have met him. Now I have my own secret."

He wandered from room to room. Dr Proctor had replaced the heavy curtain that Arabella had taken down. It was a complete castle again, with everything in its place, just the iron bars to replace. Pity about the keys. The keys? Could they be in the casket Dr Proctor had found? There was just the smallest chance.

At Goodly Harbour there were great celebrations when three boats arrived at the jetty across the road from the police station. Looking out of his window, Sgt Huff was utterly speechless. Boodle-Smith? Noodlenutt? Dr Proctor? Mr and Mrs Glum and the two missing children? Where had they all come from? They were coming this way!

In a few moments they all piled into his office, talking and laughing and making a great noise. After the official form filling, the reporter from the *Lakesiders News* took lots of pictures and interviewed them all for their sensational story. Only the Glums from Little Rushing were not mentioned – nobody wanted to talk about *them*!

Sgt Huff was extremely put out that he had not found the missing children.

"But Nora searched every inch of the castle, she told me. There was nothing, nothing at all." He shook his head in disbelief. "To think they were there all the time. Right under our noses."

"Ah, but you see it took a special sort of thinking to unravel the mystery; to get inside the cunning mind of the duke and his devices, do you see, Huff? Military experience that's what counts!" Col Boodle-Smith explained to the seething policeman.

Sgt Huff was so exasperated he could not speak, but had to admit the old soldier had done a good job.

"Just a bit of luck the bottle with the message floated up on my slipway," Mr Noodlenutt then explained to him, apologetically. "I just acted instinctively and rushed off. Only luck, you see."

Sgt Huff tried not to glare at him.

There were still a few mysteries, of course, that no one understood… the green lemonade, and the everlasting flour for the pancakes for example, but Theo and Arabella kept quiet.

"It doesn't matter now," Theo whispered to Arabella. "Let's keep everything a secret. You know what grown-ups are like."

Annie May and Reginald were overflowing with happiness.

"If it hadn't been for that biscuit tin I would never have known," she whispered to her husband. "I'm taking it home as a souvenir."

"Yes dear, of course," replied Reginald, "it will be our secret," fearing the embarrassment of telling anyone about his wife's strange dreams.

Eventually the news spread of the children's safe return. Edna and Arnold appeared at the Lakeside View Hotel within hours, where the family had gone together to rest and calm down quietly. Nobody recognised the Glums, of course.

"Yes?" said Reginald politely, as they knocked on the door of room 501.

"It's us Reginald, Edna and Arnold! How

are Theo and Arabella? So nice to see you!" and they hugged him until he was breathless and then strode into the bedroom. Annie May couldn't believe her eyes,

"What's happened to you? You look so… different."

"Yes, well, time for a change. Life is for living and all that. Like my new hairdo?" and Edna patted her blonde bouffant and preened.

"Now," began Arnold, "it's been a difficult time, I know that, and we are sorry the children got lost – but… but…" He held his hand up as Annie May and Reginald stood up angrily.

"Wait! Wait. We would like to take you all on a cruise. Re-build the bridges, so to speak. We've booked and paid for us all to go next month, please say you'll come and join us? We are going to enjoy life from now on. Derek has been taken on full-time and is our ticket office helper, and Phoebe his wife will assist him and look after Haven's Rest. Now, what do you say? Eh?"

Reginald and Annie May were so shocked, they had to sit down. He rubbed the back of his neck trying to believe what he could see and what he had heard. Annie May burst into tears,

"How lovely! How lovely!" she kept saying.

The children could see the change in the dreadful, mean Glums. How could it have happened? They too could hear their aunt and uncle offering holidays and kindness.

"Can we go, Mum? Let us go, Dad, please!" they begged.

"Okay, okay, I expect we can. Just got to do a bit of organisation at work, that's all."

Reginald rang for tea and cakes for everyone and they sat in the bay window looking over the lake, enjoying more of Mrs Magill's finest selection of pastries and tarts.

"No shortbread today?" inquired Annie May.

"Sorry madam, that was just a special Mrs Magill sent down that day. We don't have any more, I'm sorry."

"Oh." Annie May was terribly disappointed. "And the tin? Where is the tin?"

"Don't know, madam, maybe the maid

cleared it away. Was it empty?"

"Yes, but I'd so liked to have kept it."

"Sorry, madam." And the young waiter left, shutting the door quietly behind him. Mrs Magill always had her tins returned to her; it was a firm agreement between them.

"You've got to come and see that car, Dad!" burst out Theo. "It's really something! Mr Noodlenutt promised me a ride in it. Can we go and see it now?" he pestered.

"Alright, why not?" Reginald was glad of the change of conversation and the chance of some fresh air. "Anyone else want to come for a walk?"

The Glums went home to Haven's Rest which was polished and clean, with flowers on the table. They sat in the garden with a pot of tea.

"I didn't mention our illness to Reg and Annie," Arnold told his wife. "I do hope it never, never comes back. Do you think it will?" he asked in a worried voice.

"Hope not, let it be our little secret, dear. We don't want to worry them about it do, we?"

"You're right, of course. A good holiday should set us up all right. I'm really looking forward to it."

There were many secrets kept hidden that day. Dr Proctor did find the keys of the castle in the casket, but he worried, what would happen to the wonderful building once it was opened to the public? "I think it's best kept as it is," he decided wisely, as he stood by the lakeside and threw the key into the water. "It will be my secret," he told himself as it sank slowly, spinning to the bottom.

So the Castle of Charlemagne remained hidden and empty, just as the duke had planned it. Just a few special people knew its secrets, and you know who they are. The entwined 'C's on the fireplace did not represent anybody, but were the initials of his own, unique brainchild – the Castle of Charlemagne.

# FURTHER ADVENTURES OF CROCCO AND MR NOODLENUTT

## The Whispering Falls

Crocco the submersible car, his owner Mr Noodlenutt and friend Dr Proctor become involved with a Space Scientist. The professor and his family have escaped from Russia with an incredible new discovery. Zarina, the young princess, one of the last few remaining Russian Royal family, becomes very fond of Crocco. Unfortunately Russia sends a spy to discover the secret formula and a very dangerous situation develops on the lake. A near drowning, a kidnap and a incredible shooting star happen. Will Zarina and her family be safe at last? Will the new discovery change the face of space exploration?

# ABOUT THE AUTHOR

C atherine Bond is the author of the Moon series of books. Enjoyed by young and old, the books, *Moonmirror*, *Moonglimmer*, and *Moonlighter* are set in and around Dartmouth in Devon, and feature children who embark on magical adventures involving time travel, lunar mysteries, and heroic quests.

Milton Keynes UK
Ingram Content Group UK Ltd.
UKHW020154241024
450133UK00005B/288